MAGGIE

CRAFTED WITH LOVE

SHARON SROCK

Debbie
Psalm 46:10
Sharon

A BLONDE AND A PRAYER BOOKS

This book is lovingly dedicated to Jared and Sara Emmons.
"The LORD bless you and keep you;
The LORD make His face shine upon you,
And be gracious to you..."
Numbers 6: 24-25

ACKNOWLEDGMENTS

AKNOWLEDGMENTS

I have so many people to thank this time. None of you will ever know just how much your help means to me. Maggie would not have a story without you.

Kelley Garcia, who showed me what a day in the life of a home health aide looks like. Maggie's fight with Cora is almost a direct quote. Kelley, God bless you. You have more patience than ten regular people. Your patients are blessed to have you.

Cory Taylor, single foster father. Thank you so much for taking the time to answer a stranger's endless questions about some very personal things. I admire what you are doing and the call God has placed on your life.

Amanda Pierce, a real life kindergarten teacher who instructed me in all things classroom related.

Tecumseh Chief of Police J.R. Kidney. I appreciate the insights you offered. If my arrest scene and the legal parts of this story make sense, it's because of you.

Susie Warren. Thanks for trying to show this pantser what a physical plot looks like. I hope I did our brainstorming justice.

Then we have the normal gallery of too many prayer partners to name, critique partners, Marian Merritt and Terri Weldon, my editor, Robin Patchen, and proofreaders Judy DeVries and Elizabeth Lopez. There wouldn't be a book without you. I am beyond blessed to have each of you in my life. You make my make-believe world believable.

CHAPTER ONE

MAGGIE HART SETTLED in behind the wheel of her car late Thursday evening and let exhaustion wash over her. Her head ached. Her back hurt. She looked down at the bright red welts on her arms and winced. A few of those probably needed some antibiotic cream and Band-Aids.

You did a number on me tonight, Cora.

Maggie loved her patients, felt like her job as a certified home health aid was what God had called her to do in this season of her life.

But there were days.

Even though it was Christmas Eve, she hadn't considered it a hardship to check in on old Cora Burton today. Inez, Cora's eldest daughter and primary care giver, was sick with the flu. Maggie figured she could get Cora's shower out of the way, check up on Inez, and still be on time for Christmas dinner with her babies and their foster father.

The mere thought of Randy was almost enough to take the sting out of Maggie's scalp. She reached up a tentative hand and probed the crown of her head gingerly. The resulting pain had her shoulders bunching up around her ears. Nope, still hurt like the dickens.

Eighty-nine-year-old Cora hadn't recognized Maggie today, and poor Inez was too sick to be of much help. When Maggie had gone to undress her patient, Cora had slapped and scratched as if a nest of ants was attacking. Maggie finally got her calmed down enough to get her into the wheelchair for the short ride to the bathroom, only to have Cora stretch out her arms and legs at the doorway, blocking their entry as she keened like a banshee.

"Help me."

"She's trying to kill me."

"Get away from me."

"Somebody help me."

Inez had gotten out of bed at that point to try and lend a hand. Cora had clung to her daughter like a spider monkey might cling to a tree branch in a monsoon, resisting both women's efforts to get her into the shower. Cora probably didn't weigh ninety pounds soaking wet, but Maggie still managed to wrench her back in the battle. The warm water seemed to soothe Cora's fears, and the shower proceeded without incident until it was time to dry off. Then the battle proceeded in reverse, ending when Cora grabbed two handfuls of Maggie's hair and yanked for all she was worth.

Maggie dropped her chin to her chest. She hated to admit defeat, but Cora's dementia had reached the point where she needed more care than Inez and a home health care team could provide. Not Maggie's decision, of course, but something she'd have to mention to Cora's nurse after the holidays.

The thought tore at Maggie's heart as she bowed her head over the steering wheel. These people and their families weren't just clients. In most cases, they were friends. *Jesus, please watch over Cora and Inez. Help us find Your direction and Your will in this situation. I know You have a perfect plan for everyone.*

Maggie raised her head and stared through the twilight. It wasn't quite five-thirty, but dusk came early in late December in Oklahoma. She started the car. Randy had dinner planned for seven, but he never objected when Maggie arrived early.

As if on some invisible cue, her phone chimed with a picture and a text message. Maggie swiped it open, and her smile was surely bright enough to light up the interior of the car.

In the photo, Randy wore a fluffy white Santa beard, her seven-year-old son Max sported a Santa cap, while her sweet eighteen-month-old daughter Mariah gnawed on one of the sugar cookies Maggie had taken over on her visit two days ago. The message was simple.

Christmas is coming. Don't be late.

Those three faces were Maggie's whole world wrapped up in one little snapshot of time.

"Thank You, Jesus."

She didn't know a lot of women who'd thank Jesus that her children were in the foster care program. Maggie was happy to be the exception.

Oh...it had hurt, crash-and-burn hurt, remove-your-heart-with-a-dull-scalpel hurt to have her children taken away when Mariah was barely a month old. But God had known what He was doing even as Maggie's heart had bled out on the floor. In the last year and a half, Maggie had grown as a person and a parent. Now, just a couple of weeks away from completing her CPS treatment plan, Maggie was ready to take her kids back and give them the life they deserved.

Their foster father, Randy, would be a little lost and lonely once Max and Mariah came home to be with Maggie. And she had no illusions that the transition would be pain free for her children. But if the *secret* Max had whispered to her a few days ago was true, no one would be lost or lonely for long. Tingles of anticipation zipped up Maggie's spine. If there was anything that could come close to the anticipation of getting her kids back, it was the relationship that had built between her and Randy over the last few months. God really did have a plan for everyone.

Maggie didn't bother responding to the text. She put the car in gear, eased out of Cora's driveway, and headed back towards her town, her kids, and her man.

She navigated the last curve on the old highway between Ashton and Garfield and applied her brakes as a string of red lights came into view.

"What now?" she whispered as she fell in line with a dozen other slow-moving vehicles. Red and blue lights strobed in the distance. Maggie strained her neck and peered through the darkness.

Must be an accident up ahead. And just like that, someone's Christmas went from joyous to complicated. Hopefully no one had been injured.

"Jesus," she muttered. "Please keep everyone safe." As the cars inched forward, Maggie's fingers tapped an impatient rhythm on the steering wheel. She used the time to do a mental inventory of the items she'd packed in the car before heading out on her calls that morning. Randy had insisted that he had the food covered, but there had been presents to load.

For Max, a couple of new Lego kits, a remote-controlled car, and a target shooting game that fired foam darts. Her mind scrambled for a second as she tried to remember if she'd grabbed the batteries for the car. With one hand on the steering wheel, she fished in her large bag with the other, breathing a sigh of relief when she felt the blister-packed set of D cells.

Mariah had been a little harder to buy for, but Maggie had settled on a new baby doll, a stuffed unicorn, a plastic tea set, and a personalized quilt, which Lacy, one of her fellow crafters, had graciously put together. It was an intricate pattern of blue, purple, pink, and green. The large center block bore Mariah's name. It would stay at Randy's for now, but it wouldn't be long before it graced the crib in the three-bedroom house Maggie'd rented a few weeks before.

Two more weeks, thank God, and her babies would be home. Eighteen months of parenting courses, home inspections, counseling, random drug testing, and feeling like she was jumping through everyone's hoops, but hers were about to come to an end. The process had given her much to be thankful for. Randy certainly ranked high on that list, but she was ready to get on with her life.

A sharp beam of light and a tapping on the window startled Maggie out of her daydream. She gasped, then smiled at the cop standing outside the door before lowering the window.

The cop touched the bill of his cap with the flashlight. "Evening, miss. Could I see your license and insurance card, please?"

"Sure." Maggie pulled her bag from the passenger seat into her lap and dug for her elusive wallet. "Everything all right up there? I have a little medical training if you need an extra hand." She handed the requested documents to the officer.

"Everything's fine. Just a routine traffic stop." He used the flashlight to study her paperwork. "This all appears to be in order. My partner"—he motioned to a second cop walking a German Sheppard around the car in front of her—"will be with us in a second, and we'll get you on your way."

"No problem." Maggie studied the dog. That was something else she needed to think about. Like every other little boy in the world, Max wanted a dog. She wasn't sure she was up for it.

She sat while cop number two approached cop number one for a quick exchange before taking the dog in a slow circle around her car. Maggie tapped her foot. If she didn't get a move on, her early arrival was going to turn into a late one. Maybe she should call Randy. That thought was interrupted by a single bark outside the passenger side door.

Cop number one's relaxed posture changed in an instant. "Ma'am, I'm going to need you to step out of the car."

"What...why?"

Instead of answering, he opened her door. "Step out of the car, please."

Maggie released the buckle on her seatbelt and did as he requested. "What's going on?"

The officer nodded at the side of the road. "I need you to stand over there for me."

Maggie lifted her hands in surrender and followed his instructions, watching with mounting confusion as the second cop and the dog circled her vehicle again. Another bark outside her passenger door. This time the officer opened the door while the dog pawed at the ground and whined.

Cop number one joined his partner, and Maggie took a step forward. She was stopped by a hand on her shoulder. A third cop she hadn't even seen. "Stay where you are."

Maggie watched in frustrated silence as both cops went into her car.

"I've got it," Cop number two yelled.

Frustration turned to confusion. *Got what?*

Confusion turned to bone-melting horror when little white pills tumbled from a zipper bag onto a cloth spread on the hood of her car.

"What do you have?" asked cop one.

"Oxy. No prescription bottle, about fifty pills I'm guessing."

Cop one looked at Maggie. His earlier expression of polite courtesy was replaced with one of accusation.

Oxy? Maggie finally found her voice. "Those aren't mine."

He kept his eyes on her face as he spoke to his partner. "Take him around again."

This time the dog circled the vehicle without hesitation.

Cop one approached Maggie while he pulled handcuffs from a holder on his belt. "Maggie Hart, you are under arrest for illegal possession of a controlled substance."

"Arrest?" Maggie shook herself free of the hand still on her shoulder. "You can't arrest me. I've never seen those pills before."

"Ma'am, put your hands behind your back."

"No." Maggie saw her life, saw everything she'd worked for over the last year and a half, crumble at her feet. Her kids. Her job. Randy. The collapse of her future did not happen quietly. "You have to listen to me," she pleaded, raising her voice above the noise of a dozen car engines. "There's been a mistake. Those aren't mine." *Oh God, please make them hear me. I've worked too hard.* Her mind scrambled for some sort of excuse and landed on the only possible answer.

Liz.

It had to be her.

Liz Murphy, a friend from school, who'd borrowed her car last week to go visit her sister in Tulsa. Liz, who'd left drugs in Maggie's car. Liz, who was about to cost Maggie everything she held dear.

The shaking started at her toes and worked all the way up to her head. This couldn't be happening. *What can I do? What can I do?*

SHE ROUNDED on the third cop, who still stood slightly behind her. Recognition tweaked at her. She'd seen this guy around town. Jason...Jason... The name solidified, Jason Hubbard.

"Officer Hubbard, I can explain. I loaned my car to a friend a few days ago. The pills must be hers."

Someone took hold of her hands from behind. "Maggie Hart, you have the right to remain silent—"

"No!" Maggie jerked her arms free and spun, barely able to see the cop holding the cuffs through the tears flooding her eyes. She batted his determined hands away. "Why won't you listen to me? I haven't done anything wrong."

Strong hands pinned her arms to her sides. "Ma'am, we're taking you to the station. You can make this easy or you can make it hard. We have enough to charge you with possession. I don't have a problem adding resisting arrest to it."

"They aren't mine. You have no idea what you're doing." Maggie stomped her foot in frustration. The heel of her shoe landed on officer Hubbard's foot.

She hadn't meant to do that.

"That's it."

The hands were rough this time as they clasped her shoulders and spun her around. "Possession, resisting, and assault." The handcuffs were cold against Maggie's wrists as the cops escorted her to a patrol car and placed her into the back seat.

A quick slap of the officer's hand on the roof of the car and they began to move. She stared out the window, watching as her car and every dream for her future faded from sight.

"Cook kee?"

Randy Caswell ignored the insistent voice at knee level, wrapped the aluminum foil back over the ham, and replaced the lid of the Crock-Pot. He was by no means a gourmet cook, but even he could pull off a small Christmas dinner for four, especially when he had his grandma Callie hitting back-up. It had been her suggestion to put the ham in the slow cooker, a move that even a novice in the kitchen could manage. Brown-and-serve rolls and a green bean recipe off the back of the fried onion package, plus the scalloped potatoes and the cheesecake his grandma had insisted on making for him, and the feast was complete. He planned for a special night, and he wanted the meal to complement that. A glance at the clock sent his heart into a nervous stutter. Maggie should be here soon.

"Cook kee."

This time, the request came with a bit more impatience and a tug on the leg of his jeans. Randy stooped down and picked up the toddler. "What are you jabbering about, Snooks?"

Mariah put a hand on each of his cheeks and repeated her request for the third time. "Cook kee."

"I don't think so. You already had a cookie and we're having dinner in an hour. You're a big girl. Can you wait for Mama to get here?"

Mariah's little face had crinkled in the beginnings of a toddler meltdown at the cookie veto, but as he'd hoped, her expression brightened at the mention of her mom. "Mama comin'?"

Randy would never be able to explain to another living soul just what that little face did to his heart. He loved Max and all of his seven-year-old little boy orneriness, but there was something about Mariah's dark curly hair, chubby cheeks, and adoration-filled brown eyes that had him wrapped around her little finger. The scary part was that he was pretty sure she knew it.

"Yes, Mama's coming for dinner. Max is in the living room making her a Christmas card. Why don't you go help him?"

The little eyebrows disappeared under her bangs. "Cayens"?

"Yes, he's using crayons."

Mariah squirmed in his arms. "Me down."

Randy lowered her to the floor and watched her hurry from the room. Max would not be happy to have his baby sister interrupting his project, but Randy needed to finish setting the table, and he didn't want the baby under his feet while he took hot dishes out of the oven.

There were serious jitters to overcome.

Calm down. She's expecting this. It's not like you guys haven't talked about it for months. Randy took a deep breath. True, but talking and doing were two different things.

"Dad!" Max raced into the kitchen, paper clutched in one hand, a box of crayons in the other. He skidded to a stop in his sock feet.

The boy's expression was one of disgust, and Randy could hear unhappy crying coming from the living room. That hadn't taken nearly long enough. He did not have time for sibling wars right now. Randy closed his eyes, torn between his to-do list and love. Love won. "What can I do for you, buddy?"

Max held out a piece of folded construction paper. "She messed up my picture."

Randy took the drawing and studied the meticulously drawn Christmas tree. There were randomly spaced dots that he took for Christmas lights and a bright yellow star with a happy face smiling down from the top. "That's a great picture."

"Not anymore, look." Max pointed to a couple of red lines scribbled in the corner. "It's ruined."

Randy's gaze swept past the clock and landed on the still bare table. This night might be important for him, but it was just as important for Max and Mariah. Maggie would understand if things weren't perfect when she got here.

"That doesn't look so bad. I bet we can fix it." He leaned over the table, and Max scrambled into the chair beside him.

"You think?"

"I know. Hand me the crayons." Randy felt a little like Liam

Neeson. Maybe he couldn't track down a bad guy in some shady foreign country, but he could handle the problems of an average seven-year-old. Being a kindergarten teacher had equipped him with a certain set of skills, skills he could use to right this injustice. He took the box of crayons, selected the black one, and drew a box around Mariah's scribble. Next, he took the red, drew a few connecting lines, and finished with a bow on top.

"Wow."

"See there." Randy handed the paper back to Max. "All fixed." The timer on the oven dinged. "And if you hurry, you've got time to add a few more presents under your tree. Mom will never know the difference."

"Thanks, Dad. You're the best." Max looked over his shoulder as if to make sure they were alone before he leaned in for a quick man-to-man. "You're going to do it tonight, right?"

"That's the plan."

Max's grin was triumphant as he pumped his fist in the air. "Yes!"

Randy shared the boy's enthusiasm. "Do me a favor, will you? Keep Mariah occupied while I finish up in here. We want things to be just right, don't we?"

"I'm on it." Max wrapped his arms around Randy's neck in a quick hug. "We're going to have the best family," he whispered before hurrying back to his sister.

Randy watched him go.

The best family.

Those words...those kids. He was so blessed.

And to think I almost said no.

He thought back to that moment of decision almost a year and a half ago. His first foster care assignment. Not one child but two, and one of them a baby girl not quite a month old.

It wasn't just the memory of Tait Mosley that had driven Randy to apply to the foster care program. He believed that foster care was what God had for him in this stage of his life, but even knowing that, he'd doubted his ability to meet this challenge. Who could blame him for hesitating? A single guy with a full-time teaching job. He'd gone to bed one night in the peace and quiet of bachelorhood, and the next night had him searching for day care, comforting a distraught five-year-old, and doing two a.m. feedings. Foster parents didn't get the standard six weeks of maternity leave. There had been a lot of days during those first few weeks that he'd dragged into his classroom, tempted to join his students in nap time.

With his ear trained on the front door, Randy put plates on the table and pulled the highchair out of the corner.

He'd almost said no. He'd be forever grateful that he hadn't. He'd accepted the challenge, and in the midst of chaos he'd found the people he wanted to spend the rest of his life with.

CHAPTER TWO

MAGGIE, where are you?

The silent question rang in Randy's head as he disconnected another call to Maggie's phone. He didn't bother leaving a message. She hadn't responded to the dozen he'd left already. This wasn't like her. Maggie was prompt. Even with unpredictable patients, he could almost set his clock by Maggie's schedule.

His subconscious was working overtime to provide a multitude of reasons why he couldn't reach her. Had she been in an accident? Was she lying in a ditch somewhere, clinging to life, waiting to be rescued? Patient emergency...car jacked...flat tire... depleted battery on her cell.

"Where's Mom?"

Randy turned to find Max in the doorway of the kitchen. The little guy's earlier expression of anticipation had turned to worry over the last hour, leaving deep furrows etched into the space between his brows. "You said she'd be here soon." He jerked his head in the direction of the hall. "Mariah's hungry."

Randy pulled himself back into the present and tuned into the crying coming from the room down the hall. He'd put

Mariah in her crib a bit ago with plenty of toys to keep her occupied. There had been a few minutes of grace while he'd tried to reach Maggie, but it sounded like his time was up. The kids usually ate around five-thirty. Even though he'd allowed a light snack to tide them over until Maggie arrived, it was time to feed the kids without her.

"I don't know, buddy." He held up his phone and wiggled it. "I'm trying to find her. What say we go ahead and eat?"

"But what about—?"

"I know. I'm sure she'll be along in a few minutes." Without waiting for Max to respond, he brushed past him, ruffling the boy's unruly dark hair on the way. "Let's get Mariah. She sounds like she's starving." They hurried down the hall together, Mariah's cries growing louder as they approached.

Randy had purchased his home five years earlier. It was big and sprawling, with four bedrooms and a den that could be a fifth. He'd hoped to fill it with a family someday, but at the time he'd signed the papers, that dream had seemed a part of the distant future. But God had a plan. Now Max and Mariah occupied two of those extra rooms. He secretly hoped to fill at least one more with a child of his own, one with a little bit of himself and a lot of Maggie.

Maggie, where are you?

The question continued to nag, but he had to focus on the here and now. The little girl in the last room on the left needed his immediate attention.

Mariah's room usually gave him a sense of accomplishment with its glossy pink walls and white trim. He remembered the day he'd painted it and the way Maggie had teased him about pink for a girl being an outdated cliché.

Pride wasn't a factor as he paused in the doorway. How was it possible for one child, confined to a crib, to make such a mess? Discarded toys littered the floor, along with every stitch of clothing the baby had worn earlier. She stood in the corner of the crib, clad only in her diaper, bouncing on the mattress, her face a mixture of tears, snot, and frustration. The little top knot ponytail he'd so painstakingly created a couple of hours ago was askew and barely hanging on. When she saw him, she stretched out her little hands and cried louder.

Randy picked her up. "I'm here, baby." The crying stopped immediately as she snuggled her head into the crook of his neck and popped a thumb into her mouth. He patted her back and rocked back and forth for a few seconds. "I'm sorry you're upset. You ready to eat?"

"Bites?"

The hopeful tone of the word lightened Randy's mood in spite of his worry. "Let's change your diaper and put on a shirt. We can't have you sitting down for Christmas dinner in your birthday suit." He grabbed a diaper and laid her on the changing table.

"Max, can you throw the toys in the box while I get her cleaned up?"

The little boy's sigh was epic. "I guess."

"Good man." Randy plucked a wipe from the box. Before he started with the bottom, he addressed the top. "Look at your face, Snooks. You're a mess." He tickled her belly with one hand while the other wiped away the remnants of her tears. He distracted her with a familiar game. "Who loves you?"

Mariah pointed. "Daddy."

"Where does love live?"

The little girl put both hands over her chest. "Heart."

"Who's my favorite girl?"

"Me." Mariah's voice was a wild giggle as she shouted the final word.

Finished with face and diaper, Randy scooped her up and held her high. "You sound pretty sure of yourself."

From her position over his head, Mariah gave her hand a noisy smack and blew him a kiss that never failed to melt his heart. He lowered her slowly and cuddled her close, longing for the day he could be more than a foster dad. He reached out a hand and drew Max into the embrace. *Jesus, thank You for bringing these two into my life. Protect Maggie. I know something is wrong or she'd—*

The phone in his pocket rang. Randy jerked it free. The number on the screen wasn't Maggie's, and he was tempted to ignore it.

But it could be news.

He swiped the call open. "Hello."

"Randy, it's me. I'm so sorry."

Was it possible for a person's muscles to relax and tense at the same time? Relax because the love of his life was alive and on the other end of the line. Tense because her voice was full of tears and despair.

"Maggie, where are you? I've been worried sick. The kids—"

"Listen, they told me that I don't have a lot of time and I only get one call."

"They? They who?"

"I'm in jail. They found drugs in my car. They won't listen to me."

"Drugs." Randy looked at the kids and stopped. "Give me a second." He set Mariah on the floor and handed her a toy. "Max, I need to talk to your mom. Play with the baby." He stepped out of the room and closed the door. Mariah's renewed tears followed him into the hall.

Maggie's tears echoed in his ear.

∾

Maggie's hands twisted nervously at her waist while she paced the limited confines of the cell. Her heart broke a little more with each step she took.

Was this really happening? It had to be a nightmare she'd wake up from soon.

A look at her hands proved how futile that hope was. They'd given her a wet-wipe, but smudges of the fingerprint ink remained to taunt her. Words she couldn't begin to apply to herself swirled in her head. Possession...resisting arrest...misdemeanor...at least they hadn't pursued the assault thing.

Maggie wrapped her stained fingers around the bars and sobbed as she jerked with all her might.

They didn't budge.

Of course, they didn't.

Why wouldn't the police believe her? This was going to cost her everything.

"Girl, I've got a hangover that'd make Hemingway proud. I swear, if you don't plant yourself in a corner somewhere and stop that squallin', I'm going to make you wish you had."

She turned, leaned against the barred door, and stared at the set of bunkbeds against the back wall and the older woman who occupied the bottom mattress. Maggie knew the woman's name was Vicky from the cop's snide remark as he'd shoved her into the cell.

"Got you a roommate, Vicky. Play nice."

Vicky was probably thirty years Maggie's senior with a weathered face, a sour expression, and enough alcohol on her breath to make Maggie drunk by association. Right now, she was stretched out on the bunk, propped up on one elbow, and glowering.

Maggie didn't figure Vicky would be much of a confidante, but she needed to talk to someone, and her options were limited.

"If they'd just listen to me, I'd gladly leave you to your solitude. I didn't do anything wrong."

A snarky grin split Vicky's face. "Innocent, huh?"

"Yes."

"You know they hear that a hundred times a day, right?"

Maggie rubbed her arms. It was cold in this concrete-and-steel cage, and her increasing feelings of doom and betrayal didn't help. "I'm the one time today that it's true." She went back to her pacing. "This is going to ruin everything." She rounded on Vicky as if making this stranger believe the truth would win her freedom. Tears welled as she held out her hands. "My job depends on them believing me. If I don't have a job, I'll never get my babies back." Her voice broke. "My babies. I'm so close."

Vicky sighed and sat up. "Get over here and sit your caterwaulin' butt down."

Maggie followed the older woman's instructions and perched on the edge of the lumpy cot.

Vicky leaned back against the metal frame of the bunkbeds and crossed her arms. "Spill it. I'm not going to have any peace and quiet until you do."

"I've done everything they told me I had to do, but it's not going to matter now."

"Who told you to do what?"

I can't believe I'm having this conversation. Maggie closed her eyes and slumped. "I have kids. I messed up, and CPS put them in foster care. I've been without them for a year and a half. I was supposed to get them back after the first of the year. I'd never do anything to jeopardize that. I've got to find a way to make them believe me."

"Foster care?"

"Yeah, I was on my way to have Christmas dinner with them when I got stopped. I called Randy to come bail me out. I could hear Mariah crying in the background, and I didn't even have time to talk to Max. He's such a serious little guy. He's going to be so worried."

"Who's Randy?"

"Their foster dad."

Vicky stared at Maggie.

"What?" Maggie asked.

"Were you born stupid, or did you take a class?"

"Why would you—?"

"Girl, that whole system is stacked against people like us. Don't you know that? They've got your kids, and you just gave them an excuse to keep them."

"But I didn't do anything wrong."

Vicky snorted. "Good luck proving that."

"Randy believes me. He said he'd bail me out."

Maggie caught the word *stupid* muttered under Vicky's breath. Out loud, she said, "You just keep on believing whatever makes you happy." Vicky stretched back out on the cot, shoving Maggie to her feet in the process. "Is that it?"

Maggie wrapped her arms around herself and nodded.

"Good." Vicky narrowed her eyes. "I'm going to sleep now. No more blubbering."

Maggie climbed onto the top bunk and drew the thin blanket around her shoulders. She replayed her conversation with Randy over and over in her mind. He'd sounded as if he believed her. She scooted back until her back rested against the wall of the cell, where she could keep a vigil on the door. He wouldn't leave her here... would he? She made herself as comfortable as she could while the seeds of doubt that Vicky'd planted mingled with the dread and treachery already churning in her stomach. Nausea raged and, mindful of the woman asleep beneath her, silent tears streaked her cheeks. *Randy, please believe me. Please come get me.*

~

DRUGS IN HER CAR?

Jail?

Questions without answers rattled around in Randy's head. None of this made sense. None of this jived with the Maggie he'd come to know...and love. He'd never seen anyone work so hard towards a goal as Maggie had over the last year and a half. He couldn't believe she'd risk all that work with the end so clearly in sight.

He did his best to put the questions and the need to help Maggie out of his mind while he dealt with the kids. His heart might be torn, but Max and Mariah were his first priority. Mariah was easy. This was home for her. She was too young to know any different, too young to fret because Mom hadn't shown up as promised. A fed toddler was a happy toddler. She went down for the night without a peep.

Max, not so much. The seven-year-old was fidgety and full of worries and questions Randy didn't have answers for. Maggie worked hard not to disappoint her son, and Max was very much aware that this evening had been much more than just another dinner with Mom. He wasn't taking the sudden change in plans well.

He picked at his dinner, and when Randy asked him to help clear the table, his movements were stiff and jerky. Now as Randy tucked him in, despondent tears drowned out the hope that had been so bright on his face just a couple of hours before.

"Mom's in real trouble, isn't she?"

No matter how judicious Randy had tried to be in explaining Maggie's absence, Max had picked up on an undercurrent of truth.

Randy lowered himself to the side of the twin mattress and met Max's troubled stare.

"I'm not going to lie to you, Max. I don't know what's going on. As soon as I get you down for the night, I'm gonna call Grams and ask her to come stay with you while I go see what's what."

Max nodded, but Randy could tell by his lip chewing that there was more on his mind. "What else?" he asked softly.

Max broke eye contact, and Randy was stung to see fresh tears brighten the little boy's eyes.

"You're still going to be my for-real dad, right?"

"I want that more than you'll ever know." He patted his leg. "Come here, buddy."

Max scrambled out from under the covers and crawled into Randy's lap. Unable to speak, Randy wrapped him in a hug and held him for several seconds. Once the emotion melted from his clogged throat, Randy released the embrace enough to look into his eyes. "Can I make you a promise?" He continued when Max nodded, "I'm going to do everything I can to help your mom and make us the real family that we talked about. You can help."

"How."

Randy pulled him close for another second before standing and dropping him back into the bed. Max giggled as he fell, bounced, and settled. "You can go to sleep so I can go see about your mom."

Max pulled the covers up around his chin with a pretend yawn. "OK. What else?"

"Say a prayer. God is always listening, and He loves to help us and the people we care about."

"I will."

Randy crossed to the door. One hand on the knob and the other on the light switch, he asked, "You good?"

"Yeah. I love you."

"I love you too, buddy. If you wake up and need anything, Grams will be here if I'm not." He closed the door and was dialing before he cleared the hall. His mom picked up on the second ring.

"Hello."

"Mom. Sorry to call so late, but I need a huge favor. Can you come stay with the kids for an hour or so?"

A few beats of silence met his request. "It's nearly nine on Christmas Eve. I've got a cake in the oven, and it's about thirty degrees outside. What's so important that you need me to come to your house?"

Randy filled her in with the scanty details he had. "I told Maggie that I'd come bail her out." He frowned at the soft snort that came through the phone. "Mom?"

"No."

"What do you mean, no?"

"Just no."

"But—"

"You know how much I love Max and Mariah, but as far as I'm concerned, this is an answer to prayer."

"Excuse me?"

"You heard me. Those babies are precious, but I've never understood your attachment to that woman. She's a drug addict who neglected her children. I've been praying that God would do something to open your eyes before it was too late. Now that she's proven what sort of person she really is, she can stay right where she's at, and good riddance."

Randy couldn't believe what he was hearing. He'd known his mom didn't fully trust Maggie, but her reaction was over the top, even for her. "Mom, please. She says she didn't do anything wrong. I believe her."

"I'm sure you do. You're besotted with the girl. This is an opportunity to make a clean break. I don't know why you went to such lengths to allow her to remain a part of the kid's lives."

"Because she's their mother."

"A mother who neglected them."

Randy massaged his forehead with one hand while he squeezed the phone with the other. He didn't have time to argue. Maggie had been waiting for him too long already. "Look, you and I really need to have a conversation, but not right now. I gotta go." He disconnected the call and dialed another number.

Thirty minutes later, he answered the door and let his grandma Callie into the front room. He kissed her cheek as she shrugged out of her coat. She smelled of peppermint and the floral fragrance he'd grown up associating with her. In his mind, it smelled like love. "Thank you."

She patted his face. "Not a problem. My baking is done, and your grandpa was asleep in front of the TV. Go rescue your damsel in distress. We can't have her missing our family dinner tomorrow."

Randy pulled his leather jacket out of the coat closet. "Well, if Mom has her way—"

Grandma held up a hand, silencing him. "My house, my rules. I'm sorry Sophie said some hurtful things. Your father's betrayal made a bitter woman out of her. We just need to keep praying."

Randy absorbed her words. It was good advice and the same he'd given to Max less than an hour before. "I have to run. Hopefully this won't take long."

"Take all the time you need. I brought my book."

The drive to Garfield's police station was a short one. Nicolas Black, chief of police and honorary uncle, wasn't on duty, and Randy didn't know the officer who was. He wrote a check for $365.00, the amount Maggie had given him over the phone, and handed it across the desk. "Can you tell me what's going on?"

"Sorry, I can't discuss an ongoing investigation. Have a seat. I'll go get her for you."

Ten minutes later, he stood when he heard a door open. Maggie flew into his arms.

"I knew that awful woman didn't know what she was talking about. I'm so glad you came." She raised her face and met his gaze, her voice grateful when she continued. "I'm so glad you believed me."

Believed her? Of course he believed her, he loved her. Randy wrapped his arms around Maggie as she wept her relief. He'd planned to propose tonight. Bailing her out of jail was about as far removed from that as his imagination could stretch. He closed his eyes. He didn't know what was going on, but he could already feel the tightrope between responsibility and desire under his feet. It was not a test he could afford to fail a second time.

CHAPTER THREE

"ANYTHING I CAN DO TO HELP?" Maggie's question was met with a welcoming smile from Randy's grandmother, but the look his mom sent her way could have frozen an active volcano.

"I never turn down a willing pair of hands." Callie handed Maggie a paring knife. "If you can finish peeling these potatoes, I'll work on the dressing."

Maggie took the knife. "How can I refuse that? Your dressing is the best I've ever had."

Callie laughed. "I'm glad you think so. It's a recipe passed down from my grandma. I've made a few tweaks here and there. I've been trying to teach Sophie to make it, but she's never enjoyed the kitchen much."

"That's not entirely true." Sophie's response was clipped and impatient as she diced turkey giblets on a cutting board. "I don't mind the kitchen. It's the dressing. I've never cared much for it, so why learn to make it? It would probably taste like straw."

"But you're an amazing cook, Sophie," Maggie said. "I've always enjoyed dinners at your house."

Sophie's knife clattered to the cutting board. "Hang on to

those memories." Randy's mom left the chore half-finished and stormed from the room.

The kitchen was quiet for several seconds. Maggie forced back the tears that blurred her vision and threatened to turn the potato peeling from a routine chore to a blood bath. She clutched the knife and leaned against the edge of the counter. Tension between Maggie and Randy's mother was nothing new, but the stark rudeness of her parting words was an anomaly that left an already emotional Maggie sucking in deep breaths to assuage the sting.

I guess I don't need to ask where she stands on my guilt or innocence.

I won't cry... I won't cry...

"Here, let me have that before you cut yourself." Callie pried Maggie's fingers from the knife. "I know it's pointless to apologize for the actions of another person, but I'm sorry. That was uncalled for." She slipped her arm around Maggie's shoulders and pulled her close.

The fragile dam around Maggie's emotions crumbled, and she turned to lean into Callie's embrace.

"I'm the one who should be sorry." Maggie's voice broke, and she swallowed before she continued. "Maybe I should just have Randy take me home. I don't want to ruin your day."

"You're not ruining my day, sweetheart. It's Christmas. I learned a long time ago that Christmas is about more than food, presents, or even family. Now you clean your face while I go have a word with my daughter.

Maggie held tight to the older woman. Randy's grandma was one of the kindest and wisest women she knew. She looked up into Callie's bright blue eyes. "Please don't do that. It'll only make a bad situation worse. I'm fine, really."

Callie pulled away. "It chaffs me, but if that's what you want, I'll let it go. For now. I don't tolerate rudeness in my home." She cupped Maggie's face in her soft, weathered, age-wrinkled hands. "You are loved, Maggie. Always remember that. I'm sorry you're going through this, but keep trusting. I'll be seventy-three on my birthday, and in all my life I've yet to see God fail one of his kids."

Maggie leaned her forehead against Callie's. "Thank you for that, and your hospitality. I don't understand what's going on, but I just want to celebrate Christmas with my babies." Her voice faltered. "Even if I don't have any gifts for them."

Callie stepped back, yanked a paper towel from the holder over the sink, and handed it to Maggie. "No gifts? You've been shopping for months."

Maggie wiped her face, retrieved the knife, and turned back to the cutting board. She attacked the potatoes with the vengeance of an ax murderer. "Yeah, and they are all locked in my car, locked in an impound yard, closed for Christmas Day and then the weekend. It'll be Monday before I can get to anything."

"Oh, my." She peered around Maggie's shoulder. "A little less enthusiasm there if you don't mind. Let's cook them before we mash them."

Maggie forced herself to focus. "Sorry."

"That's a girl." She patted Maggie on the back. "Don't you worry. There are enough gifts under our tree for Max and Mariah to spoil four kids. Once everything opens back up, you can have a second Christmas with them. I'm sure they won't mind opening presents on a second day. You just might start a new tradition."

Maggie focused on the chore at hand for a few minutes and allowed everything Callie had said to soak in. She hadn't done anything wrong. This would work itself out. It had to. "Thanks, Callie, I appreciate you more than I can say."

"You just remember we love you, and you hang on to second Corinthians four, verses eight and nine. You'll get through this."

Maggie searched her memory and came up blank. "I don't know those verses."

Callie slid the dressing into the oven and moved to finish the giblets. "We are surrounded on every side by trouble, but we are not crushed. We are perplexed but not given to despair. We are hunted down but not abandoned by God. We may get knocked down, but we are not destroyed. My memory isn't as sharp as it used to be, so that's a Callie paraphrase, but the intent is there. There was a time in my life when that promise was all that got me through. It worked for me then, and it will work for you now.

∼

RANDY LUNGED TO HIS FEET. "Throw the stupid ball!"

"Throw it, throw it, throw it." Max echoed from his place on the floor in front of the TV."

Granddad chuckled from the recliner. "You guys afraid you picked the wrong team?"

"Not on your life, old man." Randy sat back down. "You only have a three-point lead. Arkansas is going to cream those beggars from Ohio."

Granddad chuckled. "You wish. Don't worry about your hands, though. Your grandma uses that gentle dishwashing soap, and she probably has an extra set of rubber gloves for the small fry."

"Oh, man..." Max grumbled.

Randy grinned and fished in the bowl of snack mix for another piece of his favorite melba toast. Absent their favorite rivalry between Oklahoma University and Oklahoma State University, the guys had settled on the Camellia Bowl for their

Christmas Day entertainment while they awaited the feast. Games never passed without some innocent wager between him and his granddad. Loser washed the winner's car. Loser changed the winner's oil. Today the stakes were a little higher. The loser had to wash the dinner dishes.

"That's what I'm talking about." This time it was Granddad on his feet. "Run for it son, run for it."

Randy watched in horror as an Ohio player intercepted a pass and ran it back twenty yards before being tackled. Despite his brave words, this wasn't looking good. Maybe he could find an open store during halftime and grab some paper plates.

Randy's mom stepped into the room holding a drowsy Mariah.

Randy frowned at her. Since Maggie was helping with dinner, Randy had child watch duty. He'd put the toddler down for a nap half an hour ago. When he'd checked on her during the last commercial break, she'd just been drifting off. Now Mom had her.

She took the rocker in the corner and bundled the little girl close. "You guys might want to hold it down. Mariah's trying to sleep."

"This is a war zone, girly," Granddad said. "If you want quiet, you should probably take Miss Precious back to the bedroom."

Mom frowned and continued to rock. Her attitude from last night had not improved. When he'd come in the door with Maggie and the kids, his mother had hugged him, kissed Max on the top of the head, and then plucked Mariah out of Maggie's arms without a single word of greeting. He was going to have to talk to her. But he believed in picking his battles. That hadn't been the time or place for such a touchy conversation. Instead he'd helped Maggie off with her coat, grateful for the warm welcome she'd received from his grandparents.

Wonder how Mom got out of kitchen duty?

When the next commercial break rolled around, Grandad picked up his half-filled glass of iced tea and drained it in a single gulp. He held up his empty glass and put on a crestfallen face. "My glass must have a hole in it."

Max caught the hint and jumped up. "I'll get you some more, Granddad."

Randy drained his soda and grabbed his grandfather's empty glass. "I'll get it, buddy. Stay put." He hadn't seen Maggie since she'd disappeared into the kitchen to help with dinner, and something about Mom's presence was giving him an itchy feeling on the back of his neck. This would give him a good excuse for some reconnaissance without being obvious.

He moseyed into the kitchen. Man, it smelled good. Spices and warm meat and sugar baked in about a dozen different desserts. Maggie and Grandma were busy slicing, dicing, and chopping. Their conversation seemed to center on the merits of using brown sugar instead of white sugar in homemade cinnamon rolls.

Randy drew in a shallow breath of relief, glad to see that his misgivings had been premature. Maybe Mom had decided to behave herself after all.

"Unless you're here to lend a hand, get out." His grandma spoke without turning around, her words infused with humor.

Randy ignored her. He'd heard that warning at least once every Christmas for as long as he could remember. He went for the ice dispenser in the door of the fridge and filled Granddad's glass.

The feelings of gratification he'd just enjoyed crashed and burned when Maggie turned to take something out of the fridge and he caught sight of her red eyes and the streaked makeup that had been perfect when they'd walked in the door. The ice rattled in the glass as his hand shook in fury.

There was no way Grandma had put that look on Maggie's face.

Maggie glanced up at him and gave him a slight, wavering smile. Randy met it with one of his own. It took every bit of his willpower not to storm back into the living room and confront his mother.

Oh, but he wanted to.

Instead he mouthed an *I love you* to Maggie, completed his errand, and returned to the living room.

Mom looked up at his entrance. She raised her eyebrows over a thin-lipped expression as if daring him to say a word.

Randy handed Granddad his drink and settled in his chair. Silently, he moved a confrontation with his mother to the top of his post-Christmas to-do list.

"Here you go, Max." Sophie held out another gift. The little boy, knee-deep in discarded wrapping paper and bows, waded through the mess to take the box.

"Thanks, Grams." He sat and tore through the red-and-white wrapping and flipped through the coupon booklet before looking up with a puzzled smile. "Movie tickets?"

"Yes, sir. I have one just like it. Special days out, just you and me and an extra-large bucket of popcorn. You up for the challenge?"

"You bet. It's the best gift ever."

The smile and the words warmed Sophie's heart, even if he had said the exact same thing about nearly every gift he'd opened. Gifts that she noticed did not come from his mother. Just like that girl to use her son and his family to provide a Christmas for her children that she was too stingy to provide on her own. That, and Sophie was sure that Randy had used his own funds to bail the woman out of jail. Why couldn't Randy see that he was being used? She sent a scathing look in Maggie's direction before letting her gaze settle on her son.

Randy was doing such a great job with these kids. She'd had her doubts about the foster dad thing as well as his choice of career. Who'd ever heard of a single foster dad? And the only time she'd ever heard of a guy teaching kindergarten was in an old Arnold Schwarzenegger movie. She supposed his memories of Tait Mosley and her son's lifelong soft spot for kids and wounded things influenced a lot of his choices. Regardless, he'd excelled where she'd doubted.

But the love he had for these kids went beyond the predispositions of childhood. She saw it in his every action, heard it in his every word. As much as Randy loved them, Sophie loved them more. Max and Mariah were her grandchildren just as surely as Randy was her son.

Randy was not Sophie's only child. Her daughter, April, lived in Maine with her husband, Jeremy. They had a little girl, but the job Jeremy had taken with an up-and-coming law firm didn't give them a lot of time for travel. Sophie was lucky if she got to see her granddaughter a couple of times a year.

Her youngest son, Trent, was still looking for a woman who suited him. Sophie wasn't sure he'd ever find her, considering the way the Air Force kept him moving all over the world.

Max and Mariah had filled the grandchild gap in Sophie's life. She watched as the kids moved from person to person and present to present with bright smiles on their faces and happiness oozing from their pores.

Wounded things?

Well, maybe in the beginning, but Randy's love had healed the raw parts of their lives, and if Sophie had her way, that horrible woman who called herself their mother wouldn't get the chance to re-open those wounds.

"Oh wow…" Max breathed.

Sophie's attention jerked back to the gift opening as Max sat back on his heels in front of a huge box.

"You like it?" Randy asked.

Max ran his hands over the smooth, glossy finish of the sled. "It's way cool."

"Just wait until it snows," Randy said. "You haven't seen cool until you've experienced a Caswell snow day. Sledding, snowmen, snow ice cream. Epic." He raised Maggie's hand and kissed her knuckles. "It'll be a new tradition for us."

Sophie ducked her head as the two of them made puppy eyes at each other. The whole thing made her stomach ache.

Mariah unwrapped a large stuffed bear and whooped with joy. "Lookie." She stood and turned to take it to Maggie.

"Come here, darling. Show it to Grams."

The little girl did an about face, slipped on the paper, and fell on her diaper-padded bottom. Her tears filled the room.

Maggie and Sophie both rose to comfort the baby, but Sophie got there just a second sooner. She picked the baby up, ignored the what-the-heck look from the young mother, and turned her back on Maggie. Smiling triumphantly, Sophie returned to her chair and held the child and the bear snuggly despite Mariah's struggle to get loose. "That's right, baby. You know who loves you best, don't you?"

Sophie pretended not to hear the soft gasp from across the room as an idea formed in her head. An idea that would see an end to Maggie's motherhood charade. Maybe Harrison Lake, longtime friend of the family and now in-law, could offer her some legal advice.

Christmas continued to unfold around her as she stared off into the distance, visualizing her calendar for the next week. She could make time to speak to the lawyer. Oh, yes, she could.

CHAPTER FOUR

MONDAY MORNING FOUND Maggie pacing the office of the car impound lot. She looked at her watch, concerned about the time. She needed to get to the hospice office to speak to her boss as early as she could. She needed to present her version of the weekend happenings before the *street* version reached her, and the street version *would* get there. It was just a matter of time.

She looked up as the burley attendant parked her car and came back into the building. He laid her keys on the counter and consulted his computer.

"That'll be three hundred and fifteen dollars."

Maggie's hand froze in mid reach. "Excuse me?"

Three hundred and fifteen dollars. Towing fees, three days' storage. It adds up fast. Sorry."

Maggie took a deep breath. The guy behind the counter seemed like a nice enough man. She didn't think he was out to wreck her morning. He was running a business. This was his job. The internal reassurance didn't really help.

Instead of reaching for the keys, Maggie brought out her wallet, dug for the single charge card she allowed herself for emergencies, and handed it over. Her eyes closed in a silent prayer as he swiped it. *Please, let it go through...please, let it go through.* She needed her car, but she'd wanted to give her kids a good Christmas this year, and she hadn't quite stuck to her emergencies-only rule.

"Sign here."

Thank You, Jesus. Maggie opened her eyes, scribbled her name on the bottom of the receipt, and grabbed her keys. The morning was ticking away, and she felt like she was getting further and further behind. She'd blown off the Monday morning meeting at Crafted with Love. She'd apologize to Ember and her fellow crafters later. Truth be told, she wasn't sure how to face them right now anyway.

They loved her, and they'd supported her through the last eighteen months of work and angst. But her feelings were fragile just now. If she saw a flicker of doubt on one of their faces, she wasn't sure how she'd handle it.

Any sense of relief about getting her car back with minimal problems died when she opened the door and saw the mess in the back seat. Every single gift she'd debated over and wrapped with such love and care had been ripped open. Not just the wrapping but the boxes themselves.

It was the last straw in a long weekend of insults and injuries. Rage washed over her. It was a fury that went beyond tears. And a Maggie pushed beyond tears was a force to be reckoned with. She slammed back inside the little hut and pointed to her car when the guy looked up. "What is that?"

"What?"

She crooked her finger at him and pushed her way back outside, gratified when she heard his footsteps behind her. She waved at the open back door and the destruction beyond. "That."

"Looks like they searched your car.'

"I know that. I was there. But—"

"Lady, once they have probable cause to search, they're gonna search everything." He shrugged and returned to his office.

The initial shock was wearing off. Maggie took a few seconds to examine the remnants of her carefully planned Christmas surprises. Yes, the wrapping was destroyed and the boxes were opened, but it didn't look like anything was missing. She had extra paper at home. She could tape the boxes shut and rewrap them. Nothing was really lost but a little time.

Time?

She looked at her watch again and scrambled into the car. She needed to get to the office.

"Pocession of narcotics?"

Maggie looked at her boss, Sheila Forrest. "Yes, ma'am, but they weren't mine. I'm trying to get proof of that. I've reached out to the friend who borrowed my car, but I haven't been able to contact her. I reviewed my job contract last night. I know the company has policies in place for the protection of our patients, and I agree with those policies one hundred percent." She met her boss's gaze straight on and forced every ounce of sincerity she had into her voice. "But I didn't do this. You have my word."

Ms. Forrest broke eye contact, put her chin on her fist, and tapped her pen on the open calendar on her desk.

Tap...tap...tap...tap.

Maggie waited. This was a make-or-break moment. If Ms. Forrest didn't believe her, she wasn't sure what she'd do. Child Protective Services would not release children back to a parent who didn't have the means to support them, completed treatment plan or not.

What about the charges being filed against you?

Maggie shoved that thought away. She had to believe she'd get the proof she needed to clear her name. That was a battle for later. Right now, she needed to walk out of there with a job. The tapping stopped, and Ms. Forrest let out a heavy sigh.

"Maggie, you have been an exemplary employee. You are conscientious and thoughtful. Your patients and their families love you. I wish I had another half dozen just like you."

Maggie's spirits would have soared at those words, but she could hear the but coming. She slumped into her seat and waited for the rest.

"But we have the policies you mentioned for a reason."

Employee and employer locked gazes across the desk. Maggie could see sincere sadness in her boss's eyes.

"Yes, ma'am," Maggie whispered. "I know how bad this must look, but there will be a thorough investigation. I can step back from my patient duties while that takes place. I can work here in the office until this is cleared up."

"I wish that were an option. I really do, but drug involvement is grounds for immediate termination. That's a corporate rule that I can't change no matter how much I might want to."

Maggie swallowed back tears. "I understand. I appreciate you taking the time to hear me out this morning."

Ms. Forrest looked at the door of her office as if making sure it was closed before she continued. "There may be one small concession I can make for you. I don't know if corporate will agree, and I don't know how it would work, but I don't want to lose you. I'm willing to go to bat for you. Given your work record and the fact that this is an ongoing investigation, I might be able to get you an unpaid suspension until things are finalized."

Maggie weighed the pros and cons of the offer. It wouldn't help in the short term, considering she lived paycheck to paycheck and money would be tight without the regular income, but it kept her job. It kept her out of the unemployment office and, hopefully, off the CPS radar until the investigation wrapped up.

"I'll take it," she said. "If they'll agree, that is." *God, please give me something to hold on to here.*

"Go home," Ms. Forrest said. "I'll call you once I hear back."

~

ONCE MAGGIE GOT HOME, she had her own calls to make. She needed to track down Liz, and she needed to do it yesterday. That girl had some serious questions to answer and some truth to own up to. She punched Liz's number and listened to it ring until it went to voice mail.

"Liz, this is Maggie. I'm in serious trouble because of you. I need you to call me back ASAP." She disconnected the call, not sure that this message would do more good than the last one she left, or the dozen before that.

She chewed on a nail. How could doing a favor for a friend cause anyone this much trouble?

A small, inconsequential decision that, like so many others in her life, had turned on her in the end. When would she learn?

The phone rang. Maggie grabbed it up and looked at the screen. Ember, not Liz. It rang three more times while Maggie decided how to handle her friend. Garfield was a small town with a lot to offer, but like most small Southern towns, the rumor mill was a vital link in the information chain.

"Hello."

"Hey, Maggie. Just checking in," Ember said. "We missed you this morning. No one had heard from you, and I just wanted to make sure you were OK."

OK? How was she supposed to answer that? She'd missed a

very special evening with her children. She'd spent most of Christmas Eve in jail. The proposal she'd expected hadn't happened. Her boyfriend's mother had brand-new reasons to hate her. She might as well be unemployed. And she was praying that CPS wouldn't get wind of any of this until she could drag Liz into the Garfield police station and clear her name once and for all.

Oh, she was peachy.

"Maggie?"

Maggie tuned back into the phone call. Maybe the best way to handle this was with the same proactive stance she'd taken with her boss. If she told the whole sordid story to Ember over the phone and gave Ember permission to share, she'd kill two birds with one stone. She'd get her version—the truth—out there, and if any of her friends and fellow crafters had doubts, at least Maggie wouldn't be there to witness them.

"Yeah," Maggie started. "I'm sorry about this morning. I...I uh...I had some trouble over the weekend, and I've been playing catch-up all day." She gave Ember the high points of the story. By the time she reached the part about the unpaid suspension, there were tears that she couldn't have stopped on the threat of bodily harm.

"I think my boss believed me. At least she acted like she did. I'm just... I didn't do this." How many times had she said that in the last three days?

"Of course you didn't," Ember said.

Had Ember just said that? No hesitation? No doubt in her voice?

Ember continued. "Anyone who knows you knows you wouldn't do something like this."

Ember's words rocked Maggie back on her heels. She sank into the sofa and had to swallow a time or two before she could speak. "Thanks. That means a lot."

"You mean a lot... to all of us."

Maggie absorbed those words like a dried sponge tossed into a bucket of water. They didn't make the situation any better, but to have people who believed in her? Well there just wasn't any way to overrate that. Before Maggie could form words, Ember continued.

"Can I share this with the girls? I won't if you'd rather keep it between the two of us."

"I've thought about that, and I'd rather they heard the truth from someone who knows it and believes it."

"I think that's a good idea," Ember said. "Now, what can we do to help? I don't even have to talk to the others. I know that will be the first question out of their mouths."

"I'm fine, really. Just say a prayer that God resolves this mess so I can get on with my life."

"Oh, count on that," Ember said. "One more thing before I forget. Ruthie will be back from her cruise tomorrow. I'd like to have a quick end-of-year meeting with everyone on Wednesday. Sort of an assessment of the pre-Christmas prep we did and maybe some hindsight ideas about what we need to do better for next year. Can you do that?"

"Sure. Right now, the busier I am the better."

"Probably so," Ember said. "Make me a promise?"

"If I can."

"This one is easy. If there is something you need, you'll let one of us know?"

"I will. Thanks." Maggie swiped the call closed and clasped the phone to her chest. "Thank you, Father. Even in the middle of this mess, I'm blessed."

I have a path for your feet. Trust Me.

Maggie pulled the words to her and held them close. Trust would be easier said than done right now, but it was a comfort to know that her Heavenly Father was on the job.

Maggie tried Liz's number again and got the same voice mail. She didn't leave a message this time, just disconnected the call. God had her back. Maybe she just needed to give Him some time to work.

There's not another thing you can do right now. You need to stop focusing on the things you can't control and work on what you can. You have dinner with Randy and the babies tonight. Are you going to sit here and brood until then or are you going to do something productive?

Maggie rolled her eyes at the internal scolding, but the annoying little voice in her head had a point. She slipped her coat on and brought the damaged gifts into the house. Re-wrapping them didn't take long, and each time anger tried to boil up over the unfairness of having to do this job a second time, she was able to tamp it down by imagining the smiles on her children's faces as they ripped their way through the paper.

She stacked the boxes next to the front door and looked at the little clock in her curio cabinet. It was just after one. With no job to go to and five hours until she needed to be at Randy's for their Christmas do-over, Maggie leaned back on the couch and surrendered to the mental and emotional exhaustion of the last three days. She closed her eyes and sank into sleep like a rock tossed into a pond.

Maggie sat up thick-headed and momentarily lost. She looked around, unable to remember the last time she'd slept so hard in the middle of the day. She cocked her head. What had awakened her?

"Maggie, are you in there?"

Someone was at her door. She swung her feet off of the sofa and twitched the curtain over the front window out of the way. Five women were huddled on her doorstep using each other as a windbreak against the late December cold. She yanked the door open and stood aside. They tumbled in as a single entity.

"Are you OK?" Ember asked. "We've been knocking for five minutes."

"And we've been freezing for four and a half," Holly added.

"I fell asleep on the sofa."

"Sleep." Lacy gave Maggie a long look, shaking her head. "I'd say died."

"And you'd be close," Maggie said. "What are you guys doing over here anyway?" Heat rushed into her face. She blew out a deep breath. "I did *not* mean that the way it sounded." She held out her hands. "Here, let me take your coats."

"We won't be here that long," Sage told her.

"Ember told us what happened this weekend," Piper added.

"We wanted to see for ourselves that you were OK," Sage said.

"Thanks, guys, but really, like I told Ember, I'm fine. Well, fine is a stretch, but as fine as I can be under the circumstances."

"And to that end"—Ember reached in her bag and retrieved an envelope—"we wanted to bring you this."

Maggie took it. It was the sort of envelope Ember used to distribute their end-of-month checks for the crafts they sold through her shop. "It's not payday yet."

"Well no, but close enough," Ember said. "There's just three days left in the year, and Christmas was good to us, so I made out the checks a little early."

Something wasn't right in this whole thing. Each of her friends was trying way too hard to look innocent. Maggie opened the envelope and gasped. The amount written on the check was four times the amount of the check she'd received this time last year. She knew the jewelry she made for Ember's shop was popular, but it wasn't *this* popular. She handed it back to Ember. "That's not right. Even if every piece I made sold, that wouldn't be right."

Ember folded her hands behind her back. "Every piece you

made did sell. Like I said. Christmas was good for us. We want you to have this. It's our Christmas gift to you."

"Guys, I can't—"

"Yes, you can," Piper said. "Would you cheat us out of a blessing?"

Maggie pressed her lips together, barely containing the tears that pricked at her eyes. She looked away from her friends.

Lacy touched Maggie's arm. "I know it feels big, but we love you big."

"And really," Sage assured her, "the part that's above what you earned isn't so much when you split it six ways. We want to help."

Maggie looked at the check again. It really was an answer to prayer, but it felt like she was taking advantage of the people who loved her.

"You missed something." Ember looked pointedly at the envelope.

"What?" There was nothing else in there.

Ember took the envelope and looked inside. "I could have sworn..." She handed the envelope back and fished in her bag. "Here it is. Sorry. Pregnancy brain." She held out a piece of folded paper.

Maggie took it. It was a printed email from Ruthie with a single line of text. *Take the money.*

"We are all in agreement here," Piper told her. "Let us help you."

They were killing her. She loved each of them, but they were killing her. If she was careful, this would be enough to get her through the month of January. Surely this whole misunderstanding would be over long before then. Very slowly she folded the check and tucked it and the note into her pocket. The morning's thought that one of these women might judge her filled her with shame. "I love you guys."

"Now see, that wasn't so hard." Sage took off her gloves and held out her hands. "Let's say a prayer before we go. God has a plan, and I know He's going to bring you out of this smelling fresher than a Christmas poinsettia."

Once the women had linked up, Sage led them in prayer. "Father, we give You thanks for Maggie. We love her, but we know You love her more. This situation did not take You by surprise. You hold the truth in Your hands. Give Maggie the strength she needs to wait on You. Let there be swift answers. This we pray in the name of Your Son, Jesus."

Whispered amens surrounded Maggie, and each of the women pulled her into a hug and offered private words of encouragement before she went out the door.

Maggie stood at the window and watched them go. Ember Abbott, Piper Goodson, Lacy Fields, and Sage and Holly Hoffman. She added Ruthie Gates to the list even though she was still out of town. Some of the best crafters she'd ever known. The best friends she'd ever had.

Sophie took a seat in Harrison Lake's legal office late on Monday afternoon. "Thanks for making time for me, Harrison. I know it was short notice."

"Not a problem." Harrison leaned his elbows on the desk. "What can I do for you?"

"I'm here to get some information for my son. As you know, Randy is a foster parent. The mother of the children he's raising is proving to be unfit. We need to know what to do to start the adoption process.

CHAPTER FIVE

EVEN IN CHAOS, life had its little moments of perfection. Maggie wrapped her fingers around a cup of hot chocolate and allowed the warmth radiating from the mug to melt a bit of the frost in her spirit. She wasn't forsaken, abandoned, or alone, not as long as she had her kids and Randy. Not as long as there was a great big God on her side. She believed He had a plan for her life. He'd find a way to work this out for her good, and one day, when they were a family, they would look back at the last few days and marvel.

Maggie snuggled back into the sofa and leaned against Randy's side. His arm settled around her shoulders, and she felt his sigh of contentment as they watched *their* kids at play.

Max and Mariah had finally opened their gifts. Three days late, re-wrapped packages, battered boxes underneath the festive paper. None of that had mattered. In the end, it was all about the smiles. Now that the ripping and tearing was complete, Max crawled along the floor, working diligently to shape the Lego pieces into an obstacle course for his new race car. Across the room, Mariah had her new baby doll in a toy highchair, feeding her a snack from the plastic tea set.

After the last three days, this was truly beauty for ashes.

Thank You, Jesus.

While Maggie contemplated her blessings, Mariah stood, a plastic cup balanced on a plastic saucer, tongue peeking from the corner of her mouth in concentration as she started across the room. Her course took her right through the middle of her brother's makeshift track. Her shuffling feet sent multicolored blocks skittering in every direction, destroying thirty minutes of intense construction.

"Mom..." The word left Max's mouth in an angry cry as he dropped his head into his hands.

Mariah reached the sofa and held up the cup. "You drink."

Maggie took the cup and pretended to drink. "Oh, that's good, baby, thank you." She handed the cup back, but Mariah shook her head.

"Daddy drink."

Randy took the cup and mimicked Maggie's actions. "Thanks, Snooks, you're a very good cook, but you messed up your brother's project."

Mariah took the cup and went to stand next to Max. "Me sorry." She leaned in to give him a sloppy kiss on the cheek before offering him the cup. "Drink too?"

Max wiped slobber from his face with a shrugged shoulder, irritation plain in his every movement. Before he could say anything snarky, Randy came to his rescue. "Want some help rebuilding?" He motioned to the tiled dining room. "I think we'd have better luck on a hard surface. Carpet is for sissies."

Maggie squeezed Randy's hand as he stood. "While you guys do that, I'm going to pick up all this trash and put the dishes in the dishwasher. Then it's going to be bedtime."

She ignored Max's groan. Her son would still be building at midnight if he had his way. There was a budding engineer or architect underneath that seven-year-old exterior.

Despite every promise to herself to keep her mind on the positive, once Maggie's hands were wrist-deep in hot soapy water, her mind went back to the ups and downs of the last few days.

How could it not?

The terror of being arrested, the humiliation of the hours she'd spent locked up, and the horror of Vicky's words.

"Girl, it's a system. Don't you know that? They've got your kids and you just gave them an excuse to keep them."

Maggie was so thankful that she didn't have to worry about that. Her caseworker, Samantha Archer, didn't know about the arrest. Maggie'd debated contacting her but couldn't see the benefit of piling that issue on top of the rest. She hadn't done anything wrong. Surely this would be resolved before telling Samantha became a necessity. Deep in thought and busy with the chore, Maggie jumped when strong arms circled her from behind.

"I love you."

The soft rumble of Randy's whispered words stirred the hair around her ear and tickled the sensitive skin of her neck. She repressed a little shiver of delight. Not just at the words but at the promise they conveyed. He believed in her. He'd stand by her. She leaned against his solid frame and looked at him over her shoulder. "Thank you."

He leaned back, his smile just a little puzzled. A simple thank-you was obviously not the response he'd expected.

Maggie dried her hands, turned in his embrace, and touched the side of his face. There weren't words to express what was in her heart, but she hastened to try. "You've been so good to me. I've heard horror stories about the foster care system. I'll admit that I didn't know what to expect when the kids came to live with you. I was so hurt and lost, but you rescued me right along with my babies. You made the choice to allow me to be as much a part of their lives as I wanted and needed to be. You gave me time with them even when I knew it interfered with your schedule. You included me in your plans and parties and outings. Not seeing them every day, not being the one to tuck them in every night... It's been hard. But from day one you worked to make it about the four of us. I never once felt like I was on the outside looking in. So, thank you. I love you for that."

RANDY LEANED his forehead against hers. "I think I fell a little bit in love with you that first visit. You were so nervous and doing your best to hide it. So...sincere in your determination to do whatever you had to do to get Max and Mariah back home with you where they belonged. I've never seen anyone work as hard as you have. As much as I love you, I'm even more proud of you."

He pulled her close and buried his face in the dark mass of her hair. Something sweet and floral filled his nostrils as he breathed her in. His thoughts went to the ring sitting in its wrapped box in the corner of his sock drawer. Every fiber of his being wanted to drop to one knee on the kitchen floor and ask her the question that would send their lives down the path they'd both been dreaming of for months.

He wanted her here, in his heart, in his home, in his bed for tonight and all the nights that followed. He wanted her laughter to be the first thing he heard every morning and her lips to be the last thing he tasted every night. He wanted her car in the garage next to his because it belonged there and not just because it was convenient on nights like this when the weather turned frigid.

She was innocent. He knew that with all his heart, but...

It was that annoying *but* that kept him silent. As much as he loved Maggie, asking her to be his wife before this miscarriage of justice was settled would be selfish on his part and possibly disastrous where Max and Mariah were concerned. It would be the same sort of rash decision that had cost him so much years before. He couldn't repeat that mistake.

Maggie shifted in his arms. "What's wrong?"

Randy forced his brooding thoughts aside and put a smile on his face. He took a step back, took her hands, and clasped them to his chest. When her dark eyes met his, he saw every dream he had for his future mirrored in their depths. The ring flashed through his mind a second time, tempting his resolve. It was almost more than he could handle.

"Absolutely nothing." He raised her hands to his mouth and kissed her knuckles. "I was just thinking about how much I love you."

Her chin came up the slightest bit and her eyelids fluttered closed. It was all the invitation Randy needed. This time when he pulled her close, he lowered his lips to hers in a kiss that went from gentle to scorching in the space of a heartbeat. Her hands came around his neck, and she laced her fingers in the short hairs at the base of his head. Heat exploded in his middle as conscious thought fled, threatening to take the last shards of his self-control with it.

"Yuck." Max stood at the doorway.

The word might as well have been a bucket of cold water dumped on his head as Maggie jerked away. She lowered her head to his chest. Her breath came out in a long, slow, unsteady exhale. When she finally looked up, laughter and need mingled in her eyes.

"Yeah," he whispered. "Thank God for the small fry." Louder he said, "What's up, buddy?"

"You guys are gross," Max declared before pinching his nose

SHARON SROCK

with two fingers. The other hand pointed to the living room. "Mariah has a problem."

They stepped away from each other, the moment completely shattered by the realities of parenthood.

"I'll get it," Randy said.

"No, let me," Maggie insisted. "I'll get her ready for bed." She held out a hand to her son. "Come on, Max, you can pick out a book while I get her cleaned up."

Randy watched them go.

Whew!

He pressed his lips together and looked at the ceiling. *Jesus, please work this out as fast as You can. I gotta be honest. I don't know how much longer we can keep a safe distance between us.*

He loaded the dishwasher with the plates and cups that Maggie had rinsed. While his hands worked, his mind focused on the sounds from down the hall. Mariah's sleepy whines. Max's wheedling for a later bedtime. Maggie's good-natured denial, and finally the sing-song words of a favorite Dr. Seuss book. For a few moments, he could pretend that his dream was a reality.

Finished with the kitchen, he turned off the light and started back to deliver goodnight kisses. A knock at the front door sidetracked him. When he pulled the door open, his mother rushed into the room as though pushed by the winter wind that had dried leaves swirling and chattering on the lawn.

Randy stepped out of her way before she could bowl him over. Of all the people he might like to see just now, his mother was not on the list. He loved her, wouldn't hurt her feelings for a million bucks, but her treatment of Maggie on Christmas infuriated him. He still hadn't decided how to handle her escalating resentment.

His mother didn't seem to notice his reticence.

She aimed a kiss at his cheek and shrugged out of her coat in a single motion. She held it out to him and moved past him into the living room. "Sorry to stop by so late and unannounced. Are the kids down for the night?"

"Yeah, but—"

"Good." Mom's voice went from a low don't-bother-the-kids whisper to her normal speaking voice as she sat on the edge of the sofa and leaned toward him. "I got some information today, and I couldn't wait to share."

How could she just breeze in here after the way she'd behaved this weekend and act like it was just any other day? He tilted his head and studied the woman he'd known all his life. Something in her expression put him on his guard. He suddenly wanted her out of his house before Maggie could overhear whatever it was that she'd come to say.

She rushed ahead without giving him the opportunity to stop her. "After everything that happened over the weekend with that horrible woman, that criminal who calls herself Max and Mariah's mother—"

"Criminal?" Anger lit every nerve ending in Randy's body. The heat of it overrode his caution. "What are you talking about?"

"She's a felon with a criminal record."

He clinched his fist at his sides, leashed his fury, and answered his mother with every ounce of self-control he had. "No, she isn't."

"They took her kids. Same thing."

"Involvement with Child Protective Services doesn't mean she has a record." He pinched the bridge of his nose. "Where are you getting all of this?"

"I don't have to *get it* from anyone. They don't take children from competent parents."

"You might be surprised."

She ignored his words and continued. "I spoke to Harrison today."

Their lawyer? He could only imagine the story his mother had told their old family friend. "Why would you speak to him about any of this?"

"To be ready and prepared when the time comes. You're going to need all the ammunition you can get if you plan to adopt those kids before that woman can get her hands back on them."

Of all the... Randy swallowed, so overcome with rage he could barely speak. "You need to leave."

"Sweetheart, I know you have feelings for this woman. I wish you had exercised some better judgment there, but what's done is done. Right now, you have to think about the children. She's a drug addict. I know she's claiming innocence, but you can't believe her."

Randy moved to the couch, took his mother by the arm, and pulled her up. "It's time for you to go."

"I'm only trying to help." She leaned in close as if sharing a secret. "Don't let this situation become another Tait Mosley moment."

The mention of Tait and the fact that her thoughts were tracking right along with his infuriated him. "I know what my responsibilities are. I don't need your help."

She jerked her arm away from him. "Don't you dare speak to me like that. I had my doubts about this whole foster-care thing from the beginning, but I went along with it."

"Went along...? I'm a grown man."

"Then act like one." She opened her bag, pulled out several sheets of paper, and shoved them into his hands. "Harrison wasn't much help. He said there was nothing we could do until CPS terminates her rights."

"Then what's all this?"

"Some stuff I found on the internet. Some things to watch for...things you can use to push the process along if they hesitate." She wrapped a hand around his wrist. "Put the babies first."

A soft sound from the hall reached Randy's ears.

Maggie.

Dread settled over him. He'd been so angry...so frustrated. How could he have forgotten she was just down the hall? How much had she heard? He opened the door, tossed his mother's coat around her shoulders, and practically shoved her through it.

"I love you, Mom, but I need you to stay out of my business."

When her mouth came open to speak again, he closed the door in her face, turned the lock, and leaned against it. What was he supposed to do now?

CHAPTER SIX

ADOPTION?

The word reverberated around Maggie like something from an echo chamber at a carnival funhouse. Yes, they'd discussed adoption for the future. It was a sure bet neither of the slime balls who'd fathered her children would put up a fight, but it had always been *we* not *he*.

Randy wanted her kids?

You're going to need all the ammunition you can get...

Was he going to be watching her every move now, trying to build a case against her? She couldn't stop the gasp that escaped her throat.

Maggie had leaned against the wall and strained to hear the rest of the conversation. The voices faded, and she jumped when the door slammed shut.

How could he?

So much for believing in her. She wrapped her arms around herself and bent double as betrayal body-slammed her. As bad as it hurt, there was a part of her that wasn't surprised. He wasn't the first man to stomp on her heart.

"Maggie."

She heard him whisper her name, and if it hadn't been for what she'd overheard, she might have believed the concern laced through his voice. But she'd been on the receiving end of sweetly deceptive words too many times. When he put a hand on her arm, she jerked away.

"Don't touch me." She straightened and faced him, his features almost indistinguishable through the blur of her tears. "How could you do this to me?" She brushed past him, intent on getting out of the house before the dam around her emotions completely shattered.

Randy followed.

"What did you hear?" he asked.

Maggie whirled. "Enough. Enough to know that I've been a fool...again." She swiped at her eyes and met his gaze. "You want to know what I didn't hear?" He remained silent and she continued. "I didn't hear a word from you in my defense." She crossed her arms and looked past him, convinced that the sorrow she saw building on his face had to be a lie.

Didn't it?

"The man I gave my heart to. The man I wanted to build a future with. The man I thought I could trust when all the others left me standing in the cold, stood there and let his mother condemn me without a single word of objection."

"Objection?" Randy took a deep breath. "I just threw my own mother out of my house."

"Yeah, but you got what you wanted first." She motioned to the batch of papers still clutched in his hand. "Adoption?" Maggie pulled her eyes back to his, anger mingling with despair. "I trusted you. Would you really try to take my kids without giving me the chance to prove my innocence?"

Randy kept his eyes steady on hers as he lifted the papers and tore them in half. "I didn't ask for this. I don't even know what I just ripped up, and I don't care." He released the papers, and they fluttered to the floor as he took a step forward and put his hands on her shoulders. "Maggie, you have to believe me—"

"Why should I when you don't believe me?"

He ignored her question and continued. "I have no idea what my mom was thinking, but she wasn't acting on my request. There are times since my dad moved out that I worry about her sanity. I'm sorry if you feel like I didn't take up for you. She caught me by surprise, and then I was so angry I was afraid to tell her what I thought, afraid to say things I might regret. She's still my mother."

Still? Such a little word with such huge implications. Maggie knew about *still*. Her heart might be bleeding from a fresh betrayal, but despite what she'd just heard, she *still* loved Randy. If only there was a way to make him understand what his love meant to her.

Share the truth with him.

She'd been telling him the truth for days. If he didn't believe her, there wasn't anything else she could do.

The whole truth.

"Look," he said, "I'm sorry. I love you. I—"

She held up a hand and paced away. The room around her seemed to melt away as she turned her focus inward and examined the words.

The truth shall set you free.

Maggie recognized her Heavenly Father's voice when she heard it, but what He placed in her heart usually made sense. The whole truth? That was a really ugly story short on happy endings. How could that truth help this situation?

"Maggie?"

She turned when he whispered her name. He looked a little lost and a little scared. She could identify with those feelings. Right now, her heart was hammering out of her chest. Was this the moment her two-part tragedy of a life earned its third, and final, act or could it be the beginning of a completely new story?

The fact that she had two children with two different fathers was no secret. But the details, the hurt and betrayal... She hadn't shared those with anyone. Was it time to change that? If Randy knew the whole story, would he understand how much his love meant to her?

How she'd never do anything to put what they had at risk? If she trusted him with her past, would he trust her for their future?

Maybe he'll take what you tell him and find a way to twist it to his advantage. Maggie didn't want to believe that. How could her mind be as torn as the papers scattered around their feet?

He must have seen the indecision on her face and thought it applied to him. He held his hand out to her. "Please, don't walk out the door with this between us. Tell me what I have to do to earn your forgiveness."

It was a make-or-break moment. A time to trust or walk away. Maggie chose trust. She stretched out her hand and laced her fingers with his. "I'll forgive you if you can forgive me. I'm sorry I jumped to conclusions." Her throat ached with emotion as she swallowed. "I haven't had the best luck where men are concerned. My heart always seems to get ahead of me, and I end up paying the price when everything falls apart."

This time, when he tugged, she went into his arms willingly. "Can we sit for a while? I need to tell you how Max and Mariah came to be."

Randy's expression was sincere as he looked down at her. "I've always known there was a story, but every time we got close to it, I could see the hurt in your eyes, and I didn't want to push." He led her to the sofa and pulled her down beside him.

Maggie's heart melted when he lifted her hand and brushed a kiss across her knuckles.

"I don't need to know about the person you used to be," he said. "I fell in love with the person you are."

The sweetness of his words drained the last of her anger and reminded her just why she loved this man so much. From dealing with a toddler meltdown to handling his mother, Randy was thoughtful and careful in everything he did. He always took the time to process information before he made decisions.

Randy continued. "I'm here for you if you're ready to get it off your chest."

Maggie squeezed his hand before she pulled hers free. She leaned forward, clasped her hands between her knees and stared at the floor, searching for the best place to start.

"I met Max's father when we were both juniors in high school. I was the sheltered only child. Cameron was the motor-cycle-riding, leather-jacket-wearing wild child. I wasn't a Christian back then. Neither were my parents, but they had a standard I was expected to live up to. Some of my earliest memories involve me running headlong into the wall of their expectations and falling flat on my face in my effort to circumvent what they wanted for me. I can be pretty stubborn."

Randy mirrored her pose. When she glanced in his direction, his blue eyes twinkled and his perfect smile flashed in quick amusement. "Say it isn't so."

Maggie ignored his attempt to lighten the mood and resumed her study of the carpet. "I've never understood why Cameron even noticed me in the first place, but the day I closed my locker and looked up to find him smiling down at me... Well, that old cliché about your heart skipping a beat? I think mine must have skipped five." She glanced at Randy a second time. "He's got nothing on you though. When you smile at me, my heart doesn't skip, it melts."

"I melt your heart?"

Maggie didn't miss the satisfied tone in his voice. "As if you didn't know." She bumped her shoulder against his. "Anyway, Cameron and I started hanging out before class and going to lunch together. He was the first guy to really pay any attention to me, and I fell hard. My parents were less than enthused, but I couldn't have cared less about their opinion. Cameron asked me to our junior prom. I said yes, but my parents said no. I went anyway. I told my parents that I was spending the night with a girlfriend. I went over there early, and she helped me get ready. She loaned me her dress from the year before and did my hair and makeup. Makeup I wasn't generally allowed to use."

Maggie remembered the way she'd looked that night, innocent and grown-up at the same time. The confidence had been a heady thing for a girl used to living on the sidelines. "I'll never forget that night," she whispered. "I was feeling all my oats after a few sips of Cameron's spiked punch. When he suggested we leave and go to a party, I went willingly."

She paused and picked at a rough cuticle. "I guess he got what he wanted because we broke up the following week. We were only together that one night but I found out that one night is all it takes. Owning up to my actions three months later when I had to tell my parents I was pregnant was the hardest thing I've ever done."

"How did they react?"

"They supported me, at least outwardly. I guess having a pregnant daughter in their home was less embarrassing than tossing a pregnant daughter into the street. But something broke that day that we've never been able to fix. We became polite strangers living in the same house. I was barely seventeen and just starting my senior year in high school. But I got a job and once the baby was born. I never asked them for a thing. Not a package of diapers, not for babysitting while I worked or studied, nothing." She shrugged the old nagging pain away. "I haven't spoken to either of them in a couple of years. They may as well have disowned me for all the warmth they've shown."

"I'm sorry you went through that. And Cameron?"

Maggie laughed, but there was no merriment in the sound. "I haven't seen him since the day I refused the money he tried to give me for an abortion. Last I heard, he was out west some-where, living on a ranch, playing at being a cowboy. He's never seen Max, and as harsh as it sounds, we're both better off without him."

"He doesn't pay child support?"

"Nope." The brown leather of the sofa creaked as she pushed herself off the cushion and went to stand by the big bay window. She twitched the curtain aside and stared out into the dark. "I don't need indifferent parents, and I don't need a reluctant man."

"Stubborn and independent?"

Maggie turned and folded her arms. "Six of one, half a dozen of the other. Maybe it's good that we're having this conversation. You should probably know what you're getting into."

RANDY WATCHED Maggie pace the room after that final state-ment. Nervousness radiated off her like heat waves off asphalt under a hot summer sun. What did she expect him to say?

"I like a little backbone in my women."

Maggie spared him a wide-eyed glance.

Didn't expect that, did you, sweetheart? He leaned back and crossed his arms. Parts of her story were killing him, but some-thing told him she wouldn't appreciate his sympathy, so he led with curiosity. "Tell me about Mariah's father."

The wistful expression that flitted across Maggie's face had jealously roiling in his gut. In an effort to redirect that energy, he stood. "I need a soda, you?"

"Sure." Maggie followed him to the kitchen and took a seat on one of the bar stools at the island. Her fingers stroked the smooth granite, absently tracing the thin vein of gold that ran through the beige. Randy handed her a glass and watched as she stared into the tiny bubbles popping over the top of her drink.

"Jack Baxter. Ten years my senior and everything I thought I wanted in a man. Max was two when I met Jack. Despite the theme of countless romance novels, there aren't a lot of men lining up to take on the responsibility of a ready-made family. Jack was different. At least I thought he was. He and Max became buddies at first glance. I had to almost force him to plan a date night without Max tagging along. If for no other reason than that, it was impossible not to love him. Like I said, he was older. He had a stable job, and he knew what he wanted out of life. That he wanted me and Max was a dream come true."

"Your parents had nothing to say about that?"

"What could they say? I was nineteen and master of my own destiny. Besides, they liked Jack." She shrugged. "Did they like Jack for being Jack, or did they like Jack for being willing to take me and Max off their hands? That's a tough call, but when Jack suggested we move in together, they seemed more than happy to help me pack."

Maggie sipped her drink before continuing. "We were pretty happy for a couple of years. Max loved having a dad and I loved making a home for the three of us. It felt like I'd finally found my fairy-tale ending."

"What happened?" his question was a whisper. He might not know the details but the fact that Maggie was in his kitchen instead of Jack's told him that the answer wasn't going to be pretty.

Maggie was silent for so long that Randy feared she was done.

"I found Christ." She picked up her drink and emptied half the glass in one gulp. When she set the glass back down on the bar, she clasped her hands around it and stared into the depths. "Jack encouraged me to go to college. I didn't know what I wanted to do with my life, but I signed up for some basic courses. Most of it was online, but I had in-person classes one night a week. One of my classmates was a Christian, and we became friends. When I look back on that meeting, I see God's fingerprints all over it. Meeting her changed my life in unimaginable ways. She encouraged me to get my certification for home health care, and she invited me to church."

"You said your parents weren't Christians. Had you ever attended?"

"No, but something inside of me really wanted to go. I asked Jack to go with me, but he laughed it off, said he'd had all of that lifestyle he wanted when he was a kid. But he didn't try to stop me from going. I loved it. There was something...electric in the air." Maggie put a hand over her heart and met Randy's gaze. "Something my heart wanted without my head being able to explain it." She chuckled. "I still can't put it into real words."

"You're doing a fine job."

She drew in a deep breath before she continued. "I got saved on my third visit, and God immediately began dealing with me about my living arrangements. Jack and I needed to get married if we were going to continue living together."

"You'd been together for a while by then. Marriage never came up?"

"Just in passing. But those discussions always ended the same way. What we had was special. We didn't need a piece of paper to reinforce that to us or prove our love to the world."

Randy held his breath, His heart breaking for the girl Maggie'd been.

"I tried to explain what I was feeling, but Jack didn't see it that way. I tried to override the constant ache in my spirit, but God wouldn't be ignored. I loved God, but I loved Jack too." She swallowed, and her voice quivered when she continued. "I didn't want to choose. I didn't know how to choose. We loved each other, and with him, Max had a dad." Her words faded to a whisper and ended on a sob.

"We can stop now if you need to," Randy said.

"No, I'm almost done." Maggie tore a paper towel from the roll on the bar, wiped her eyes, and continued. "Jack and I rarely argued, but that changed. It seemed like we were at odds more than at peace. I came home from class one night and he was in a romantic mood. I just...couldn't. He gave me an ultimatum. Him or God. He left the next morning on an extended business trip. I don't think he expected me to make the choice I did, but when it came down to it, it wasn't really a choice."

"A step of faith?"

"The biggest of my life, and God made a way. I didn't have money for my own place, and my parents weren't going to welcome me back. But, Peggy...the friend who'd invited me to church. She offered me space in her apartment until I could finish my courses and find a job. The home health care thing turned out to be a huge blessing at that point. Those courses take months, not years. I moved out of Jack's house, and my first night on that lumpy sofa bed was the best night's sleep I'd had in weeks.

"When Jack came back and found us gone, he called and tried to convince me to come home. When I mentioned our need to get married, he hung up on me. I tried to reach out to him when I realized I was pregnant, but I couldn't find him. It was as if he'd dropped off the face of the earth. I had Mariah seven months later. You pretty much know the rest."

She met his gaze from across the bar, and the fresh tears in her eyes tore at him.

"I told you all of that because I want you to understand how much what we have together means to me. I haven't always made the best choices, or been the best person, but what you and I have matters. You have to believe me when I tell you that there is no way I'd jeopardize that. If I can clear my name—" Sobs cut off her words.

Randy came around the bar and gathered her into his arms. Thoughts of the hidden ring circled in his head. Images of Tait joined in. Randy had zero doubt that Maggie was telling him the truth but he refused to allow himself to make the selfish choice. He had to put Max and Mariah's safety first.

"I'm sorry you went through all of that, but I'm not either of those men." He held her close. "When I say I love you, I mean it. I'm not going anywhere. Tell me what I can do to help you prove your innocence."

CHAPTER SEVEN

MAGGIE PARKED BEHIND CRAFTED with Love at seven-thirty Wednesday morning, turned off the car, and picked up the cake plate from the seat beside her. She was going to have to get back to work if for no other reason than to protect her waistline.

Her churning emotions and uncertain future were making her fidgety. When she was fidgety, she crafted or she baked. Between her continual failure to reach Liz and her emotional evening with Randy on Monday, she was doing both. Yesterday she'd made several beaded bracelets along with three of the sea glass necklace-and-earring sets that had been in such high demand for Christmas. She'd baked eight dozen chocolate chip-oatmeal cookies to drop off for Valley View's youth service tonight, plus the cake she had in her hands. At least when it came to the calories generated by her nerves, she was spreading the love.

She lifted the lid of the cake carrier and filled her lungs with the scents of cinnamon, nutmeg, and pumpkin. This pumpkin bread recipe was her grandmother's, and it was simply the best she'd ever tasted. She hoped the girls agreed because this wasn't just a random treat. It was her way of saying thanks to the friends who'd been such a blessing to her over the last few months. Friends whose constant encouragement was priceless. Friends whose recent generosity insured she could make it through the next thirty days.

A quick glance at the alley told her she was the last to arrive. She'd let Ember know last night not to stop for donuts. Her co-crafters would be looking for breakfast to go with their coffee.

"There she is," Ember said as Maggie pushed her way through the door.

"What did you bring us?" Holly asked as she rushed to grab the heavy door. "I'm on my third cup of coffee this morning, and I need something to soak up the caffeine."

Sage, Holly's sister, smirked at Holly's remark. "You're always on your third cup of coffee. Give the girl some space."

Ruthie lowered her cup onto the table. "I swear, the way you two snipe at each other. If I didn't know you were sisters, I'd know you were sisters. You remind me of my daughters. We had a grand time on our Christmas cruise. They may be grown but they still bicker like kids. There was never a dull moment between the younger one telling the older that she could smell her freckles and the older reviving a favorite, less than complimentary, nickname."

Maggie put the cake plate on the table and moved in to give Ruthie a welcome-home hug. "Look at you with a winter tan and sun-streaked hair. I think it's great that you got to have some time with your daughters. I'm glad you had fun, but it's good to have you back home."

Ruthie patted Maggie on the back. "Those two girls of mine gave me a week I'll never forget, but home was a welcome sight."

"No shipboard romance to report?" Lacy asked.

Ruthie actually blushed at the question. "I'm too old to kiss and tell." Then in an expert move to change the subject, she turned to Holly. "I hear congratulations are in order. Let me see."

Holly held up her left hand and buffed her new ring on the front of her shirt before holding her fingers out for Ruthie's inspection. "News travels."

"Yes, it does," Ruthie said as she examined the engagement ring. "It's lovely. Riley has great taste."

"What? Let me see that." Maggie leaned over Holly's hand while a hint of jealously sparked. It should be her showing off an engagement ring, would be but for Liz. She squashed those thoughts and looked at her friend. "Why didn't I know about this?"

"She showed it to us on Monday," Piper said. "Oh..." The word was a drawn-out sigh. "You weren't here."

"Sorry," Holly said. "Riley asked me to marry him on Christmas Eve." She wiggled her fingers. "I guess my happy news got lost under your bad."

"And that pretty much brings us full circle," Ruthie said. "You girls have been busy while I was away. Catch me up."

"I think Maggie has to get us started there." Ember put a stack of paper plates on the table, took the lid off the cake, and started slicing pieces. "This smells heavenly. I can tell before I've tasted it that I need the recipe."

"I can get that for you," Maggie said. "As for fresh news on my situation, there really isn't anything new to report. My case won't go before a judge until after the New Year, and I still can't reach the friend who borrowed my car. Ex-friend," she amended.

"Bless your heart," Ruthie said. "I know they suspended you from your job. How is Randy handling all of this?"

Maggie stared into her cup, wondering how to answer that question. Randy was being as sweet and as thoughtful as ever, but there was something happening that she couldn't quite put her finger on. He claimed to trust her, promised to help in whatever way he could, but she sensed a hesitancy in him that hadn't been there before.

She could understand why Randy hadn't acted on Max's couldn't-keep-it-to-himself secret on Christmas Day, but there'd been plenty of opportunity since. She'd thought surely it would happen Monday night, especially after everything she'd told him. *Not* that she'd shared her past to sway him, but his continued hesitation both confused and hurt. Maybe she was imagining it. Maybe the whole thing with his mother was skewing her impressions.

Randy's mother.

As happy as she was to be spending some time with her friends, as determined as she was to put Sophie's meddling out of her mind, the thought ripped the Band-Aid off and laid the fresh wound bare. Her hands trembled as she set her plate aside. "Randy would handle it fine if his mother would mind her own business." The words jumped out of Maggie's mouth before she had a chance to temper them.

"Oh, that doesn't sound good," Lacy said.

"It isn't good," Maggie said. "That woman had the nerve..." Sophie's behavior on Christmas Day combined with Monday night's episode and congealed in Maggie's stomach. The resulting knot of resentment made it hard to breathe. "You guys know that Randy means the world to me, but there are days when it's hard for me to imagine the sweet-tempered man I love coming from such a spiteful witch." Maggie pressed her lips together and reminded herself that the *spiteful witch* was going to be her mother-in-law soon, God willing. With a conscious effort, she unclenched her lips and blew out a cleansing breath before propping both elbows on the table and resting her head in her hands. "Sorry, that was uncalled for."

"Sometimes we need to vent," Ruthie said. "As much as you

love Randy, I imagine it's hard to be honest with him where his mother is concerned."

"She makes me so angry," Maggie whispered.

"Better to spill to us, I'd think," Lacy said.

Ember reached across the table, took Maggie's hands in hers, and lowered them to the table. She held them gently but didn't speak until Maggie lifted her head to meet her gaze. "We aren't after the latest gossip. This is a safe place. What you say here, stays here."

"And we can help you pray." Holly was the youngest of the crafters next to Maggie, and a new Christian. Her soft words were just a bit tentative, as if looking for approval from the rest of the group.

Sage put a hand on Holly's shoulder. "My little sister is absolutely correct. We'll take it straight from your mouth to God's ears."

Maggie allowed her gaze to roam the table. She wasn't used to such acceptance. How had she been so blessed? When she looked in the mirror, she saw a pregnant-at-seventeen, two-baby-daddies, never-married, drug-addicted screwup.

These women looked at her and saw a friend.

I see a daughter, beloved and treasured. A daughter I have good plans for.

The gentle reminder robbed Maggie of words and filled her eyes with tears.

"Oh, none of that." Piper shoved a napkin across the table. "You'll have us all blubbering."

Maggie freed her hands from Ember's grasp, picked up the napkin, and dabbed at her eyes. "Randy's mom has never been my biggest fan. When we're together, it's more polite tolerance than anything else. This whole thing hasn't helped that. Witch is an ugly word, but it fits her behavior at Christmas. Even more so after Monday night." Maggie had to pause to take several ragged breaths.

"Don't stop now," Holly said.

Sage forked up a bite of cake and handed it to Holly. "Stuff this in your face and hush."

The sisters' antics made Maggie grin. She took a bite of her own piece of cake, chased it with a sip of coffee, and continued. "Randy's mom came to his house Monday night. She didn't know I was there. Randy insists that I park in the garage now that the weather has turned so cold. I was putting the kids to bed when he let her in. She'd..." Maggie forced out another exhale in an effort to steady her voice. "She'd been to see a lawyer. She was there to give Randy the information he needed to..." Her voice broke, and she didn't know if she could even say the next words out loud.

"To do what?" Lacy prodded.

"To take my kids away from me." The words left Maggie's mouth in a whoosh.

"Do what?" Ember words fell out of a slack-jawed mouth.

"No way," Holly said.

"Dear Lord, be with us now," Ruthie whispered.

"No..." Sage closed her eyes, and her lips moved in what Maggie assumed to be a prayer to go along with Ruthie's.

"Randy wouldn't do that." Piper was the principal at the school where Randy taught. Her words were brisk and sure. "I work with him every day. He wouldn't do that."

"You're right. He didn't." While Maggie's hands twisted the damp napkin to shreds, she relayed the story of what she'd over-heard and the heart-to-heart conversation that followed.

She told them the whole story of the bad choices she'd made and the betrayals she'd suffered at the hands of Cameron and Jack. By the time she finished, most of her friends had their own napkins in their hands.

When she paused to take a breath, Piper wiped her eyes and motioned around the table. "Told you so."

Maggie grinned in response. "Yes, you did. You guys don't know what it means to have somebody...six somebodies so eager to listen and support."

Ember rose and crossed to the counter to retrieve the coffee pot. When she returned, her smile was a little sad. "Some of us do."

"That's a fact," Holly said, her head bobbing in agreement.

"You guys are the best. I know this isn't why we came here today, but I need to finish the story," Maggie said.

"There's more?" Lacy's question was incredulous.

"Just a little," Maggie said. "You guys have been so supportive and trusting. I know you've had questions about how I lost my kids. Ember knows what happened. I was upfront with her when she took me on as a crafter, but other than Randy, no one else knows the whole story."

"I'd be honored to be trusted," Ruthie responded.

The others nodded their agreement.

When the coffee carafe came her way, Maggie topped off her cup and looked at the far wall for several breaths before she continued.

"After I moved out of Jack's house and realized I was pregnant, again, I was scared to death. I wasn't sure what I was going to do. Jack had disappeared, I was living on a friend's sofa, just getting ready to complete my courses. My friend Peggy was so sweet. She insisted I stay right where I was until I got established in a job and had some regular income.

"I moved into my first apartment, a little two-bedroom hovel, just a couple of weeks before Mariah was born. I brought the baby home and began the work of making a home for the three of us. I thought I was on the right track for the first time in my life."

She looked at her friends, unsure how to explain what was in her heart. "I know that making babies outside of marriage is wrong, but I loved them so much. I know God forgave me for my past. I refuse to call either of them a mistake."

"Of course not," Ruthie exclaimed. "God promises us beauty for ashes. I think unplanned children are the best example of that."

"Thanks," Maggie whispered. "I've had so many people make me feel like I should apologize for their existence." She swallowed. "Anyway, there I was, barely twenty-one with two babies to support, standing on the edge of a busy career and hoping to take that career a step further. I was back to work two weeks after I gave birth, coming home exhausted, trying to give my children the time they deserved and still taking the online nursing courses. I wanted that nursing degree so badly I could taste it. If I had that, I could give Max and Mariah a solid future."

"You gave up those courses a couple of months ago, didn't you?" Ruthie asked.

"Yes, ma'am."

"What changed your mind?" Holly asked, then slumped in her chair when Sage sent her a withering glance. "Sorry, ignore me. It's none of my business."

"I don't mind. A couple of things fed into that decision. One, I love the job I'm doing so much more than I ever imagined. My patients have become extended family, and they need me. I feel like I've found God's niche for me right where I am. Second, I took a long hard look at my schedule. There is no way I could continue doing work, school, and crafting once Max and Mariah come home. That's what got me in trouble to start with."

"How so?" Piper asked.

Maggie looked down at the table. Would they condemn her for her past? *Please, God, help them understand.* "What I'm about to say isn't an excuse for my screw-ups. I just want you to see where I was."

"No one's here to judge you," Lacy said.

The words bolstered Maggie. "Thank you." She sipped her coffee and forged ahead. "Max was such a good baby. He hardly ever cried unless he needed a bottle or a diaper change. I got spoiled and wasn't ready for Mariah. She was colicky and never happy. Between her lack of a schedule and my regimented one, I wasn't getting any sleep. I was coming in late to work every other day. The morning my boss called me in for an on-the-record counseling session was the day I knew something had to change. I couldn't afford to be unemployed. I went to the drug store and found something guaranteed to make me sleep. Problem was, I was so dopy in the morning, I needed something to wake me up, so I stocked up on that as well. It was a vicious cycle that got out of control fast. I never took anything that couldn't be bought over the counter, but I can't imagine an illegal drug addiction being any worse."

"You poor thing," Piper said. "You must have been exhausted."

"Beyond exhausted. The first time the cops came banging on the door at midnight because Mariah was crying and I hadn't heard her, I was so ashamed. They told me a neighbor had called, concerned about the baby. They looked around but seemed satisfied when I told them that she was just fussy and I was a heavy sleeper. I wasn't so lucky the second time they got called out three days later. That time, they called child protective services. I was a wreck, the apartment was a mess, I hadn't had time to shop in a week. There was food in the kitchen... but not a lot. CPS decided that the kids needed to be moved to a safer environment while I got my act together. It was the worst day of my life. I'd be lying if I said I didn't question God in all of that. How could a Christian, doing everything she knew to do, end up in such a devastating place? But God had a plan. He used Randy to turn my devastation into something beautiful." She closed her eyes, her heart breaking on the next words. "God keeps telling me that He has a plan for my future. I'm doing my best to hold onto that promise, but I'm going to lose everything if He doesn't work a miracle real soon."

CHAPTER EIGHT

"Doin'?"

The toddler's question drew Randy out of his work zone just before lunchtime on Wednesday. He straightened and grimaced as the kink in his back let go. His third-quarter lesson plan lay scattered across the wooden surface of the dining room table like birdseed on snow. He wasn't nearly finished, but he'd made progress.

Some people might think that teaching kindergarten was the easy way out when it came to a career in education. Some people had never spent the first week of school with half their class in tears as they struggled with separation anxiety. Some people had never spent the first semester of the year trying to convince a room full of five-year-olds that he was not their mother. They really could wipe their own noses, tie their own shoes, and keep track of their own backpacks. Add to that the responsibility of teaching them colors, numbers, letters, shapes, and hopefully, that glue was not a food group, and well... He had news for *some people*.

Christmas break ended on Monday. So much had happened over the last week that work had been relegated to the bottom of his priority list. He'd allowed Mariah to fall asleep on the sofa after breakfast, hoping she would take an extra-long nap while Max enjoyed a play date with a friend, but the first lesson he'd learned in parenting was that you didn't always get what you expected.

Mariah came to the table in her footed pajamas, holding her new doll in one arm and dragging her favorite blanket behind her. She boosted up on her toes so that her eyes came even with his work surface.

"I color." She dropped the doll to reach for the colored highlighters Randy was using to color code his plan.

"I don't think so." Randy scooped her up, plopped her in his lap, and bent her back to expose her chubby tummy. "I'm going to take a bite right here." He blew raspberries on the exposed skin while Mariah squirmed.

"Yum...yum...yum!" Each *yum* served to increase the volume of the toddler's shrieks of laughter. He finally sat her up and held her close while they both caught their breath. He rested his chin on her disheveled dark hair and scooped the papers into a tidy stack that he'd finish later. "Did you have a good nap?"

Her little shoulders jerked in a quick shrug. She might be a toddler, but she was smart enough to know she probably shouldn't admit to enjoying nap time.

"Down." She shimmied out of his lap. "Fursty."

"Juice?"

"Yes!"

She took one of his hands in both of hers and tried to pull him to the refrigerator. He groaned as he straightened. His backside was asleep and his legs were stiff from sitting in one place for too long. "I think you saved me, Snooks. I was about to become one with the chair."

Mariah grinned and pointed at the fridge.

He opened the door and picked her up so she could see the three bottles lined up on the top shelf. "Orange, apple, or grape?"

"Gape."

"Good choice." With Mariah bouncing up and down in impatient anticipation, he filled her sippy cup half full, screwed on the lid, and handed it to her. The first drink she took had the purple liquid running in a steady stream down the front of her shirt.

"Shoot." Randy grabbed for the cup, and the cross-threaded lid went flying. Now she wasn't the only one wearing a purple shirt.

Mariah held up both hands, fingers working while her feet did a little war dance. It never ceased to amaze him how quickly a sunny disposition could disintegrate into a meltdown, complete with real tears and snot.

"My gape..." she wailed.

He dumped the glass in the sink. "I'm working on it." It was hard to concentrate with Mount Vesuvius erupting at his feet, but this time he made sure the lid was properly aligned and screwed down tightly before handing the cup to the thirsty little girl. The sobs died immediately.

Randy leaned against the counter while Mariah sucked down half the drink. "Better now?"

She lowered the cup and gave him a luminous smile. "Good dink." She handed the cup up to him as if it had never been the focus of world peace and picked at her wet shirt. "Ucky."

"That you are, and I'm not much better." Anticipating an early nap for her and a work morning for himself, he'd left her in her pajamas, and he still wore the loose sweat pants and T-shirt he'd slept in. "What say we clean up this mess and get dressed before brother gets home for lunch? Hot dogs sound good?"

When she clapped, he knew he had a winner. He used a

damp dish towel on the floor and then opened the fridge a second time to make sure he wasn't making promises he couldn't keep. No hot dogs, but he had two packs in the deep freeze out in the garage.

Randy held out a hand. "Come with me." He led her to the front door and slipped his feet into a pair of worn slippers. A frosty burst of air hit him square in the face when he opened the door. If he took her with him, she'd freeze in that wet shirt. It was times like this that he questioned the wisdom of the original owners of his house. At some point, they'd remodeled the kitchen and removed the door that connected the kitchen to the garage. To get to the deep freeze, he had to go out and around. He didn't like leaving Mariah alone in the house, but the trip to the garage would take ninety seconds. He hit the button to raise the door.

"Wait right here, OK? I'll be back in a second." He dashed out of the house, closing the door behind him, and froze when he heard the click of the lock.

Randy turned and tried the knob to no avail. With his head against the door he considered several choice names for himself. Idiot took first place. He straightened. The lock was a simple push button that would disengage if the knob was turned from the inside. Getting Mariah to do that shouldn't be too much of a challenge.

"Mariah, open the door for Daddy." Randy jiggled the knob in futility as a second burst of winter wind whistled through the eaves. The cold was going to turn him into a Popsicle if she didn't open up soon. He pounded on the door and immediately scolded himself. Scaring the child would not get him what he needed.

"Mariah, Daddy's cold. Please open the door."

Randy waited in vain for another minute or so before backing away from the door and assessing the situation. He snapped his fingers as a memory struck. There was a spare key in the glove box of his car. With his arms wrapped around himself in defense against the cold, Randy sprinted for the garage. But when he pulled on the latch nothing happened.

Locked.

The car was never locked when it was in the garage... Well, almost never.

His breath fogged around him as he considered his options. Maggie had a key. He could call AAA for the car, or a locksmith for the house. All of those options would leave Mariah alone in the house alone for too long.

All that was left was to make a quick check of the windows. Maybe he could find one that was unlocked. At the kitchen window, he pressed his face against the glass and shielded his eyes from the glare. Mariah was sitting in the floor next to the table playing with her doll. He tapped the glass. "Snooks...baby, let Daddy in." She looked up, waved, and went back to her doll.

So much for that. At least she was visible and safe. He tried the window, not surprised when it didn't budge. A trip around the house revealed more of the same. If nothing else, he could feel safe from an outside intruder.

He went back to the kitchen to check on Mariah. She was standing on one of the chairs with his box of highlighters in her hands. It wouldn't take long for her to destroy what he'd spent all morning working on. He tapped on the window and waited until she looked in his direction. "No. Put those down."

When he heard a muffled giggle as the little girl turned away from him, Randy bowed his head. "God, I need to find a way into this house, right now." The sharp sound of a car door closing drew him back to the front yard.

Max was home from his overnight with Alan.

Yay. They could all freeze together.

He approached the car and stopped. Alan's mother was

headed to the front door with a little boy on either side. Their stiff postures had his eyebrows climbing. No one looked particularly happy to be there.

"What's up, guys?"

Alan's mother froze in mid-step and turned, her hand over her heart. "Oh, my goodness, you scared me to death. I was just about to ring the bell. I didn't expect you to come up behind me."

"Sorry," Randy said.

The woman tilted her head and studied Randy. "You're practically blue. What are you doing out here in nothing but a T-shirt...a wet T-shirt?"

Randy explained his dilemma. "The baby has been in there, by herself, for nearly twenty minutes. I can see her, she's safe, but she won't open the door. I'm about to try breaking a window."

"Oh no—"

"Grownups are so dumb." Max pulled away from the woman, bent to reach under a denuded shrub, and pulled out what looked to be a good-sized rock. With a quick motion, he twisted it in two, dumped a key in his hand, and handed it to Randy.

When he did, Randy got a good look at his face. His lip was split at the corner, and there was a smudge of blood around his mouth. He took the boy's face in his hand and looked from Max to Alan's mother. "What happened?"

In response, the woman forced her son's face into the light to reveal a bruise high on his cheekbone. "We need to talk."

"Yep." Randy clutched the key in his fist. "Hopefully we can do that inside where it's warm." He shuffled around them, slipped the key into the lock, and turned it. The door opened without a protest. "Come on in and have a seat. I need to check on Mariah."

He dashed through the house and found her still standing at the table, scribbling like a madwoman. His sigh of relief was audible. She was making quite a mess, but she was doing it on blank paper. When he scooped her up, his nose wrinkled. The mess wasn't contained to the table.

Randy carried the toddler through the living room on his way to her bedroom. "I'll be right back." Thirty seconds later, the door to Max's room slammed shut.

"What the...?"

Mariah babbled as if the question was meant for her.

Randy addressed the diaper change with as much speed as he could. He took the extra seconds to run a wipe over her face and chest and changed her into a fresh outfit before hustling to his own room to grab a fresh shirt for himself. The sweatpants would have to do for now. At least they hadn't been doused in grape juice.

He hesitated at the closed door to Max's room but decided against confronting the youngster before he had the facts. He trusted Alan's mother to tell him what he needed to know, and missing out on the seven-year-old drama sounded like a good thing after the last thirty minutes or so.

Randy returned to the living room, put Mariah on the floor with a book, and faced his visitors. "Sorry for the delay. Now what happened?"

Alan's mother leaned forward in her chair. "I'm not sure of all of the details. Both boys seem to be determined to keep the cause of their disagreement to themselves. I was cleaning the kitchen up from breakfast when I heard a crash and shouting from Alan's bedroom. The boys were rolling around on the floor, pounding on each other. The crash was the little table that holds Alan's hamster cage. The cage was lying on its side, and I found the hamster cowering in a corner. Both boys have minor injuries, but poor Chubby may never be the same."

"I am so sorry," Randy said, his hands spread at his sides. "It's not like Max to fight with a friend. Can I pay for anything that was broken?"

The woman waved his offer aside. "That's not necessary. Little boys scuffle, but this looked serious. I have no idea who started the fight, but I wanted to make sure things were OK here."

Randy gave himself a moment before he responded. One would think that, after a year and a half, he'd have developed a thicker skin when it came to people doubting his role as a foster parent. He swallowed back the irritation. "Why would you ask?"

"You mean, besides the fight?" The woman sent him a concerned smile. "Max was a little sullen all evening. He seemed better this morning." She paused and when she continued her voice was a whisper. "We know there was some trouble with his mom over the weekend. I was hoping to get Max alone for a few seconds to see if there was anything I could do to help, but—"

"I punched him," Alan said.

Both of the adults looked at the little boy, sitting on an armchair with his head down.

"I punched him," he repeated, "and if he comes back to my house, I'll hit him again."

"Alan!" His mother was on her feet.

Randy stepped between them. "May I?"

The woman raised a hand in surrender. "By all means."

Randy stooped down next to the chair. He'd had Alan in class a couple of years before. Hopefully, some of his influence remained. "You want to talk about it?"

Alan reached up to touch his bruised face, his lips pursed in indecision. He cut a quick glance at his mom before looking back down at his knees. With one breath, he seemed to make up his mind. "He said Dad wasn't coming home."

"What?" His mother said.

Randy shifted his attention to her.

"My husband is out of town for a couple of days. He's due back tomorrow. What would give Max the idea that he wouldn't come home?"

Alan straightened in his chair. "That's what I said. Then Max said all daddies were liars." Alan crossed his arms and glared from his mom to Randy as if daring them to bring his reasoning into question. "So I punched him."

Randy absorbed Alan's words with a sinking feeling in the pit of his stomach. Had he been so wrapped up in what was happening between him and Maggie that he'd failed to see what was happening in the heart and mind of a seven-year-old little boy? The child he considered his own? He answered his own question with one word.

Obviously.

Randy saw his visitors out with the promise to call later with Max's side of the story. He fixed Mariah a bowl of soup and, once she was fed, he put her in her crib with several toys. He disliked confining her, but he needed to have a serious talk with Max.

"Snooks, I need to spend some time with Max. Can you play for a little while?" He took her jabbering response as agreement and left her happily engaged.

He crossed the hall and knocked on Max's door.

"Go away."

The two-word response broke Randy's heart. He and Max had developed a special relationship over the last eighteen months, one Randy hoped to nurture in the years to come. He bowed his head against the door.

Jesus, help me get to the bottom of this.

He turned the knob and let himself into the room. Once inside, he closed the door and leaned against it. Max was curled on his bed with his back to the room.

Randy cleared his throat. "I wanted to say thanks for your help getting the door open earlier. How did you know about the key?"

Silence stretched between them. Just when Randy thought Max wasn't going to answer, he rolled over and sat up. "I found it when I was playing last summer. You didn't put it there?"

"Nope. Must have been left from the previous owners. Just so you know, if you ever need it, I'm going to put it right back where you found it."

Max shrugged.

Randy held his gaze for several seconds. "You want to tell me about the fight?" he finally asked.

Max looked away and maintained his silence.

Randy asked the question that was tearing him apart from the inside out. "Why would you tell Alan that daddies were liars?"

When Max brought his eyes back to Randy's, there were tears glistening in them and his chin trembled. "Because they are." His words were broken and harsh. Once they left his mouth, he flung himself back onto his pillow as his shoulders shook.

Randy hurried across the room, pulled him into his lap, and held him while he cried it out. He hadn't dealt with such heart-broken behavior from Max since the night he'd accepted custody from CPS. That night, Max had cried for his mother for hours. This felt like more than that. Once the sobs died away, Randy kept him close, at a loss.

"I need you to talk to me."

Max sat up and wiped a sleeve across his wet face. "You said we were going to be a family. You lied."

"Buddy, that's the thing I want most in the world. Why would you think differently?"

Max scrambled out of his lap. He picked up a baseball from his nightstand and fiddled with it. The ball lost his interest, and he moved to his bookcase and flipped through the pages of a book. He seemed to be gathering his courage.

"Mom said my real dad left when she told him about me. Daddy Jack said he loved me, but he left too. You said you were going to ask Mom to marry you so we could always be together, but you didn't. It's almost time for us to go live with Mom again. Did you change your mind? Are you mad at me? Are you going to leave us too?"

Randy held out his arms, and Max ran into them as new sobs ripped through his small body. Tait and Max might be years apart, but they needed the same thing. Someone to protect them. Somehow, that was Randy's job...again. How could he explain the difference between what he wanted and the harsh realities of being an adult? The difference between his dreams and the nightmares that haunted him? He pulled Max back into his lap, and Max buried his head in the bend of Randy's shoulder.

"I'm sorry I got into a fight with Alan. I'm just afraid."

Explanations crowded Randy's mind, but he went with the simple. "I'm afraid, too, buddy, and I'm sorry. Sometimes grownups have to fix problems before they can keep promises." He shifted Max away so that he could look him in the eye. "But I'm not going anywhere. I'm not mad at you. I love you with all my heart. I promise you that if there's a way to work this out, I'm going to work it out. I want you and Mariah to be my kids forever."

Max studied Randy's face for a long time as if looking for any hint of falsehood. Obviously satisfied, at least for the moment, he snuggled back against him. "I love you, Dad."

"I love you too, buddy."

They sat that way for a long time. A soft snore from Max let Randy know that he'd cried himself to sleep. He shifted him to the mattress and closed the door softly behind him. Across the hall, Mariah was enjoying her second nap of the day. He'd be lucky if either one of them slept tonight.

Randy thought about the work that remained on his lesson plan.

"Not happening."

He didn't feel like working. He felt like hiding in a closet with a two-liter bottle of soda and a bag of chips. Adulting was hard, and he'd had all he wanted for one day.

CHAPTER NINE

*W*EAR SOMETHING *pretty but not too dressy.*

Randy's instructions circled in Maggie's brain as she stood in front of her closet Thursday afternoon and considered her choices. Medical scrubs in a variety of colorful patterns dominated the space, but beyond that, her choices were woefully inadequate.

Maggie tapped her pursed lips with her steepled fingers. Randy was taking her out for a special New Year's Eve dinner, just the two of them. A rare enough occasion in and of itself, one made difficult to plan for by his refusal to share the destination.

Maybe he had something besides dinner in mind for tonight.

Hope bubbled up inside of Maggie at the thought, but she squashed it just like she'd done every night for the last week. Every night that she'd come home without a ring on her finger. Each of those nights was a brick in a rapidly increasing wall of bitterness. All their talk of a future and a life together seemed to be stalled out since her arrest on Christmas Eve. If he believed her, why was he hesitating?

Thanks, Liz.

But what if their heart-to-heart talk a few nights before had fixed some of that? What if tonight *was* the night?

The question galvanized Maggie and had her pulling items out of the closet. She studied the results with something less than enthusiasm. *Not too dressy* wouldn't be an issue with the options in front of her. When it came to clothes, she was a mix-and-match sort of girl. Her job dictated most of her day-to-day wear, and beyond that her preferences were casual. She looked at the handful of shirts and sweaters and the pairs of jeans and leggings draped over hangers, chewing her bottom lip.

"I could have sworn I had at least one dress in there." The mumbled words were frustrated. A random flicker of memory had her snapping her fingers. "Wait just a minute." She pushed aside her work clothes and dove head first into the recesses of the long, narrow space. Two feet by eight feet. She'd measured it when she moved into the new rental three months before. The three-bedroom house had been perfect for her anticipated reunion with her kids. The no-lease part of the arrangement ideal in the face of her plans with Randy. But really, who built a closet two feet wide and eight feet long...without a light?

Maggie located the three boxes stacked in the back and pulled them out one by one. A box of baby clothes, a box of stuff from high school, and... She smiled when she removed the lid on the last carton, revealing more of her clothes. She carried it out and turned it upside down on the bed to dig through the pile. Mostly maternity clothes, but...

"There you are." The object of her search was a mid-length blue skirt with black embroidery around the hem and a high fitted waist. She hadn't worn it since getting pregnant with Mariah. It seemed as if just the mention of the word pregnant had added three inches to her middle during that first trimester.

The linen and silk would be perfect for tonight, assuming it fit. Maggie shimmied out of her jeans, crossed her fingers, and slid the skirt up over her hips. She held her breath as she reached for the short zipper and tugged. When the zipper closed without the slightest hesitation, she exhaled and hurried to the full-length mirror in the bathroom.

Maggie smoothed the fabric over her hips and stomach. It fit and even left her enough room to breathe and enjoy her dinner. She twisted back and forth, watching as the skirt flirted with her calves, and decided that her black flats would complement the look beautifully. She hurried back to the pile of clothes and began digging for a suitable top.

Nothing.

The skirt begged to be paired with something soft and black. Maggie unearthed a black sweater and immediately discarded it because it had little pills of white sprinkled all over it from an encounter with a towel in the dryer. Even her lint shaver wouldn't clean it completely.

Maggie checked the time. It was a fifteen-minute drive into Ashton. She had time to shop for something new, but she wasn't working, and the thought of being frivolous with the money her friends had given her didn't sit well. Could she justify the expense? A final look through the clothes on the bed convinced her that there was nothing suitable available. Surely, between the after-Christmas sales and the end-of-year clearance racks, she could find something in a decent price range.

She changed back into her jeans, and armed with a forty-dollar budget and the optimism of the desperate she headed off to the mall.

There was something sad about the stores this time of the year. The glitz and sparkle of Christmas remained, but the excitement in the air was missing. Shelves and racks held an adequate jumble of clothes, but they seemed to be waiting on a boost of new spirit, as if they were biding their time until the colorful spring fashions came to bring an infusion of new life.

Joyful shoppers had been replaced with long lines at the service counters as impatient customers waited to make returns and exchanges. Maggie skirted those lines with a mumbled prayer of thanks, grateful that those lines were not her destination for today.

She wandered the largely uncrowded stores and aisles, flipping through racks of sweaters and blouses. The second shop she visited yielded paydirt. A fitted sweater made of soft black cashmere that would hug her waist and complement the full cut of the skirt. The original price was eighty dollars, but that number had been slashed through in bright red ink. So had the fifty-dollar price underneath that. The current price was thirty-five dollars. Maggie stroked the sweater and considered her options. If she'd found this so quickly, what might she find in the next shop...or the next? Seemed a shame not to check it out, but if her treasure hunt went south and they sold this, she'd be kicking herself all the way home.

Maggie waved a passing clerk to her side. "Excuse me."

"Yes, ma'am. How can I help you?"

She held up the sweater. "I was wondering if you could hold this for me for a bit? I'm looking for something specific. This is close, but I'd like to look around a little more."

"Sure thing. Follow me." The clerk took the garment and led Maggie to a deserted register. After a few seconds of searching, she unearthed a pad of paper and a pen. "Name?"

"Maggie Hart."

She wrote Maggie's name on the paper, made a notation of the date, and pinned it to the sweater. "You're all set. I can hold it for you until we close for the day."

Maggie rubbed the cashmere between her fingers a final time. It really was the best she thought she could do, but there was something alluring about the hunt, not to mention an odd urge to venture back out into the mall. "Thanks so much. I'm pretty sure I'll be back way before my time runs out."

With a little more bounce in her step than she'd started with, Maggie stepped out into the mall and froze.

Liz.

Maggie watched in disbelief as the *friend* who'd landed her in this mess...the *friend* who hadn't returned a single phone call in a week...the *friend* who'd been scarcer than snow in August, strolled by on the other side of the aisle. Maggie started to call her name but decided on a more direct approach. She crossed the distance, came up behind Liz, and took ahold of her upper arm.

Liz spun, but her startled look melted into a smile. "Hey, Maggie. What's up?"

Maggie dragged Liz out of the flow of the foot traffic. "Don't *what's up* me. I've been trying to call you for days. Where have you been?"

Liz shook her arm free and smoothed her shirt before answering. "Chill, girl. My boyfriend took me to spend Christmas with his family. My phone konked, like totally D.E.A.D. I couldn't get another until I got home because the stupid cheap warranty was only good where I bought it. I was totally disconnected from the outside world for seven whole days. Archaic, but amazing. You should give it a try sometime."

"I'll keep that in mind," Maggie muttered. "We need to have a private conversation, like yesterday."

"That's why I'm here instead of home catching up on my sleep after being cooped up in Dylan's musty old pickup for sixteen hours." She fished in her pocket and pulled out a phone cased in a sparkly blue holder. "Get a load. They gave me a new number and everything. I'll give it to you, and we can have all the conversations you want." That said, Liz punched in some numbers and Maggie's phone rang from deep inside her bag.

"That's me," Liz said as Maggie reached for her phone. Liz swiped the call closed. "Now, we can talk anytime you want."

Maggie studied her friend in the less than adequate light of the mall. Liz was always a little flighty, but Maggie wouldn't have pegged her as an addict. The stash the cops had pulled out from under her seat proved what a great judge of character Maggie was. Now, what had always seemed like an amusing personality trait bore heavier significance.

Maggie leaned in close and tried to whisper above the noise. "Are you sober?"

Liz took a step back. "What?"

The confusion on Liz's face and the innocence laced in her response almost made Maggie doubt herself. But the fact remained that the pills the cops found didn't belong to Maggie, and that left only one other person. Still she hesitated.

What if...?

Grow up, Maggie. She's playing you.

That little internal voice snapped Maggie back to reality and put some iron in her spine. "We need to go someplace private."

Liz was shaking her head before Maggie stopped speaking. "No can do. Dylan's picking me up for a New Year's Eve party. I need some serious get-ready time." Her smile turned a little sappy, and she put her hands over her heart. "I think he might be ready to pop the question." She gave Maggie a quick hug, the question of her sobriety obviously forgotten. "Call me next week, and we'll have a nice long visit."

Pop the question? The words seethed in Maggie's stomach. There was little doubt in her mind that Randy would have already proposed if not for Liz's actions. She latched onto Liz's arm before the woman could make good on her exit.

"I found your pills," Maggie whispered. She took a breath

and a moment before she continued. "Let me rephrase. The *police* found your pills."

Liz's smile was just a little too bright. "Pills?"

"Don't play innocent with me. I don't have the time or the patience. I got stopped at a road check on Christmas Eve." Maggie told Liz everything in quick whispers. "I need you to come with me to the police station, right now, and help me clear this up."

Liz focused on the floor for several seconds. When she finally looked up, there was sincere regret on her face, a regret that did not translate to her words. "I'm sorry, but I can't do that."

"You can't *not* do that," Maggie insisted. "Do you have any idea of the trouble you've caused? I'm suspended from work, and if this goes to trial, it will probably cost me custody of my kids." She pushed back the tears that hovered on the fringe of her words and reinforced them with determination. "You have to tell them that they were your pills."

"I can't. I promised Dylan I was clean. If he finds out I lied to him again... He won't give me another chance." Liz straightened and put a hand on Maggie's shoulder. "You've been a good friend, and I'd help you if I could, but I can't risk it."

"You can't..." Anger shook Maggie so thoroughly that she struggled to string words into a sentence. "I don't think you get it. Whether you go with me or not, now that I know you're back in town, I'm going to tell them where to find you."

"And it will be your word against mine. I'll deny even knowing you." Without another word, Liz turned and walked away.

Maggie watched her go, disbelief warring with despair. So if Liz told the police the truth, it might cost her Dylan's love. How did that measure up against Maggie's kids, her job, and Randy? It didn't.

Maggie crossed the aisle and went back into the store. She purchased the black sweater and drove straight home. Randy had promised to help her. She had no idea what he had planned for this evening. A discussion about Liz probably wasn't anywhere on his list, but it had just made the top of hers.

~

"Oh, wow."

Randy smiled at Maggie's exclamation, the third of the night. The first had come when she'd realized that their dinner destination was the restaurant on the fiftieth floor of the Devon Tower building. The second had been a small under-her-breath mutter as they'd entered the elevator to be whisked into the heavens. Now, she stood at his side staring out the huge windows. Seven hundred feet below, Oklahoma City had become a fairyland of twinkling lights sprawling in every direction.

He tugged at her hand. "Our table is ready."

Maggie tore her gaze from the windows and sent him a beaming smile. "You said special, but this is the most amazing thing I've ever seen."

Her words pleased him. She'd been unnaturally quiet for the drive into the city. He got it. Things were still a mess, and the future remained more than a little uncertain. He'd put some soft music on the radio and allowed her some space. She was beautiful tonight. The blue-and-black outfit suited her, accenting her willowy figure. When he'd helped her into the car back in Garfield, the soft texture of the sweater felt like an invitation to hold her just so he could snuggle into the warmth. What she'd done with her hair and makeup was beautifully subtle, and he felt honored to have her on his arm. As the host led them to their table, he caught the glances of appreciation from more than one male guest. He put a possessive arm around her waist.

Eat your heart out, guys. She's all mine.

"Here we go." The host stopped beside a table-for-two next to the windows and motioned Randy to a chair on one side before pulling the other out for Maggie. Once they'd both been seated, he snapped open a pristine white napkin, laid it in Maggie's lap, and handed each of them an open menu. "Enjoy your dinner. Your waiter will be with you shortly."

Maggie laid the menu aside and scooted her chair just a bit closer to the window. "I can't get over how different everything looks from up here."

Randy reached across the table, threaded his fingers with Maggie's, and smiled. "I think I have the better view. You look amazing tonight."

Maggie ducked her head at the compliment. "Thanks. How did you know that I've always wanted to try this restaurant?"

"Lucky guess" He released her hand as the waiter stepped up to their table.

"Good evening. My name is Marco and I'll be serving you tonight. Have you had a chance to look at your menus?"

"Not yet," Randy answered. "We've been enjoying the view."

"Ahh, yes. It can be a bit distracting. May I recommend an appetizer? We can get that started while you decide."

"That would be great," Randy said.

"The Chef's Charcuterie and Cheese Board is a personal favorite of mine and a great place to start."

Randy looked at Maggie. "Is that OK with you?"

"It sounds perfect."

"Very good," Marco said. "Can I bring your drinks out as well?"

"Iced tea?" When Maggie nodded, Randy held up two fingers. "Tea for both of us."

As Marco departed, they both picked up their menus. After a couple of minutes of quiet study, Randy said, "I think I'm having the New York Strip. What looks good to you?"

"I'm torn between the lamb or the duck. I've never tried either, and they both sound delicious."

Maggie closed her eyes and jabbed a finger at the menu. It was a risky way to make a decision, but Randy watched in delight as she cracked an eye open. He could tell from her smile that she was pleased with her choice.

"I'm having lamb," she said.

"OK."

Marco returned with their drinks and appetizer, took their dinner orders, and departed once again.

Randy waited while Maggie filled a small plate with bits and pieces of meat and cheese and several pieces of toast. He did the same, and a comfortable silence settled over their table while they sampled Marco's recommendation. After a couple of bites, Randy noticed that Maggie seemed to be rearranging the food on her plate more than eating it. Something about her mood harkened back to the pensiveness he'd noticed in the car. He swallowed. "What's wrong, sweetheart? Not to your liking?"

Maggie blinked and looked at her plate. "No...this is amazing. Marco has great taste." She picked up a cube of cheese and popped it in her mouth.

"As lovely as you look tonight, I can tell you have something besides food on your mind. You might as well share it. If you don't, I'll spend our entire meal trying to guess what's bothering you."

Maggie's gaze went back to her plate. "You can always see right through me. I do have something I wanted to tell you... planned to tell you, but..." She motioned around the elegant room before meeting his gaze. "This just didn't seem like the best setting. You went to so much trouble. I don't want to ruin our evening by dragging my problems into it."

"*Our* problems, Maggie. What affects you affects me. Isn't that what love and being a couple is all about? Now, talk to me."

Maggie's gaze dropped back to her lap. When she spoke again, Randy had to strain to hear her words. "I saw Liz today."

Randy took a moment to process. "Liz?" He leaned forward and lowered his voice to match hers. "Your friend Liz, the one who left the pills in your car?"

Maggie nodded.

"Well, what did she say?"

When Maggie looked up, he saw the sheen of tears in her eyes. "Not much." She told him about her chance meeting and the end to their conversation. "She isn't going to help me, Randy. As far as she's concerned, I'm on my own. I've been a wreck all week, but I had this hope I was clinging to. That Liz would do the right thing, and we could put this behind us. That's not going to happen, and I don't know what to do."

Maggie took the napkin out of her lap and blotted her eyes. "I don't understand why God is doing this to me...to us. I know you said you'd do what you could to help, but I don't know what you can do if she refuses to tell the truth."

Fury roiled through Randy. On the upside, it was good that there was, finally, some verification of Maggie's story. Of course he believed her, but no one else would without Liz's cooperation. But that she'd spoken to Maggie in such a way... It took every ounce of control he had to keep his hands from shaking as he held them out to Maggie. "Once we're done with our meal, text me Liz's address and her new phone number. I don't know what I can do, but it's times like this when having the chief of police as your unofficial uncle is a good thing. Maybe I can get him to bring her in for questioning. He's good at what he does. If she's lying, he'll see it." He looked around the room and didn't see Marco. "Now, close your eyes."

When she did, he bowed his head over their joined hands and whispered a prayer. "Jesus, thank You for bringing us this far. We're trusting You for justice." *More justice than Tait got.* He couldn't go there. His prayer continued. "Wrap Your arms around Maggie, and let her know that she isn't fighting this battle on her own. She has You, and she has me. You can push Liz towards the truth. Help us find a way. We ask in Your name, amen."

"Amen." A voice whispered from beside the table. Randy looked up to see Marco standing respectfully to the side, a plate in each hand.

"Dinner is served," he said.

Randy's steak was medium rare and perfectly seasoned, but he barely tasted it. It was his turn to be reticent as his thoughts churned. He hadn't doubted Maggie for a moment. It was the legal system he didn't trust. A legal system that had failed a shy, young kid so many years ago. That failure nipped at the heels of his trust.

Maggie's encounter with Liz should have freed him from whatever hesitancy had plagued him over the last few days. And for a second, he wished he'd brought the ring with him. This would have been the perfect place for a proposal.

Selfish.

The word came out of nowhere and taunted him. Now wasn't the time to think about what he wanted. Until the police made a proper arrest, this situation could still go south. Max and Mariah were depending on him to protect them. He wouldn't fail a second time.

CHAPTER TEN

RANDY PULLED close to the curb the following morning, shifted into park, and allowed the car to idle as he studied the little house where Maggie's friend lived. He'd stewed all night. Not just over the things this woman, this *friend* of Maggie's had said to her, but about the best way to handle this confrontation.

Taking the information straight to Nicolas Black, Garfield's chief of police, had seemed like the logical place to start last night. But he'd learned about injustice the hard way. Sometimes, if you wanted something done, you had to take care of it yourself.

Maggie's friend was going to be in a lot of trouble once the police got wind of her involvement. Nothing he did or didn't do was going to change that. But if he could talk Liz into going to the station voluntarily as opposed to bringing the police down on her head, the authorities might be persuaded to go easier on her. At least that was the spin he planned to put on the upcoming conversation.

At this point, he didn't really care about what the police did or didn't do to Liz. He just wanted Maggie's name cleared so that they could get on with their lives. Taking this into his own hands seemed the fastest - and surest - way to get that done.

And besides, the idea of being Maggie's knight in shining armor appealed to him. The way she'd looked at him the night before when he'd reiterated his promise to do what he could to help... To say he'd liked it would be an understatement.

Randy bowed his head over the steering wheel, determined not to go one step further without his secret weapon.

Father, please give me the calm and words I need to persuade this woman to do the right thing. Soften Liz's heart. Maggie calls her a friend. Let her be one now.

With one more deep breath to bolster his determination, Randy shut off the car and took the short walk up the cracked cement path to the peeling paint of the faded front door. He knocked, then stuck both hands back into the pockets of his jacket. With his shoulders hunched up around his ears and his breath fogging around his head, he was reminded of being locked out of his house a couple of days before.

Maggie's friend didn't seem to be in any more of a hurry to open the door than Mariah had.

Good grief, it was cold. Randy stomped his feet. He could feel his toes freezing while he waited. There was a TV playing somewhere inside the house. There was a car, presumably the one that had been in the shop before Christmas, parked in the drive. Someone was home. "Come on," he mumbled, pounding the door a second time.

"Hold your horses, I'm coming."

The door opened a crack, a safety chain bisecting the narrow space. Still, there was enough room for a first impression to register. The woman on the other side was blond and quite pretty, despite her bedhead. She wore fleece pajamas. Eeyore and Piglet socks protected her feet from the cold of the bare tile floor.

"What?" Liz sounded sleepy. Made sense. He hadn't dropped Maggie off at her house until after one. It had been almost two before he'd found his own bed. The need to confront this woman and then pick Max and Mariah up from his grandma Callie's were the only reasons he was out and about on New Year's morning.

"Look, I'm letting all the heat out. What do you want?"

"Liz Murphy?"

"That's me. You've got thirty seconds before I close this door."

"I'm Randy Caswell. I think you know my girlfriend, Maggie Hart."

At the mention of Maggie's name, the woman's expression shuttered. "Sorry, time's up."

Randy managed to wedge his foot in the opening before she could close the door in his face. "Look, I just want to talk."

"I've got nothing to say to either of you. I thought I made that clear yesterday."

Randy's short supply of patience froze with the next gust of winter wind. "All you made clear yesterday was that you aren't nearly the friend that Maggie thought you were."

"Whatever. You're trespassing, and I'm asking you to leave. I'll call the cops if necessary."

Randy stared at her. "That's not a bad idea. I'm sure we could find something interesting to discuss." He ignored the pressure on his foot as she shoved on the door.

"Look," Liz said when the door refused to budge. "I like Maggie, I really do."

Randy studied the tears he saw forming in the corners of Liz's eyes, and the hope that he might have reached her spurred him on. "And she likes you, which is why she helped you when you asked to borrow her car. Don't repay her generosity like this. If they pin possession of those pills on her, pills we both know didn't belong to her, she's going to lose her kids and everything she's worked for. I can't believe you'd want that."

Liz swiped at her face with the sleeve of her pajamas. Her voice was a whisper when she continued. "I'd give a lot to be able to help her, I really would, but if I go to the cops, they'll lock me up and toss the key."

Randy bolted through the opening she'd just given him. "It probably wouldn't come to that, not if you volunteer the truth. Chief Black is a friend. If you come with me and tell them the pills are yours, I'll talk to him for you."

"Liz, who's at the door?"

Randy took an involuntary step back when a second figure came into view.

Liz's expression turned desperate. "No one, sweetheart." Her smile was obviously forced as she turned to face the new player in their little drama. "Well...obviously someone, since he's right there. He's just lost and looking for directions."

Randy met the new arrival's gaze above Liz's head.

"Can't help you, bro. I don't live in this neighborhood." He wrapped one of her blond curls around his finger as gave it a gentle tug. "Make it snappy, babe. I'm hungry, and I want to pick up my truck before it gets much later."

"Sure thing. Go start the coffee and I'll be right there. Pancakes?"

"Oh, yeah."

Liz turned back to Randy. "The Browns are three houses down on the north," she said aloud for her boyfriend's benefit. *I'm sorry*, she mouthed.

As the door began to swing shut, Randy blocked it a second time. "Look," he whispered. "Can you please just think about what I said?" He fumbled in his back pocket for his wallet, opened it, and pulled out the contact information he'd prepared before leaving the house this morning. He handed it through the narrow opening. "Call me if you change your mind."

Liz took it but didn't say another word before she closed the door in Randy's face.

~

NICOLAS BLACK LEANED BACK in his chair with his arms crossed as Randy paced in front of his desk.

"I'm telling you, Nicolas, Maggie didn't do this. I know she tried to tell your officers that the pills weren't hers. I know that everyone who comes through this office claims to be innocent. But I just came from her friend's house. She all but admitted to leaving that bag in Maggie's car. You have to drop the charges."

The other man remained quiet for so long, that Randy thought he hadn't heard a single word. "Don't you have anything to say?"

"I have plenty to say," Nicolas said. "Let's start with your foolishness in approaching this woman before you came to me." The chair squeaked as he leaned forward. "I know you probably think that was justified, but I'm not going there with you. What happened twelve years ago has no bearing on what's happening now. You're standing there all loaded for bear, but do you have any evidence to back up your claim?"

Randy stared at the son of his grandpa's oldest friend. He spread his hands to his sides. "Aren't you listening? She said—"

"What she said isn't evidence," Nicolas said. "If that were the case, most of those innocent people you just mentioned would be running around free. Everyone has someone to blame for their crime."

"But—"

"Randy, I need you to listen closely to what I'm about to say. I believe you."

Randy sat in one of the visitor chairs. He opened his mouth to express his relief, but before he had a chance to speak, Chief Black held up a hand. "Let me finish. I've known you all your life, I trust you, and more than that, I trust my gut. Right now, my gut is telling me that your girlfriend is innocent. That's the good news. The bad news is that it isn't up to me. Her case has been handed over to the district attorney, and he's the only one who can say yay or nay. His decision will be based on *physical* evidence. As it stands, we have Maggie's car with a substantial amount of a known narcotic in it. Your word, her word, the word of some invisible third party doesn't change the fact of Maggie's car with drugs in it. Do you get that?"

He got it. He didn't like it, but he got it. "Go talk to Liz Murphy yourself."

"I can't do that. At least not yet."

Randy was at the end of his patience. He'd come in so full of hope, and now he felt like he was locked in a burning building with the key to the door in his pocket, but with his hands tied behind his back. "So she walks just like those two goons..." He bit the words off and forced himself to focus on the here and now. "She all but told me she did it."

"And what if the next guy I arrest tells me that you're responsible for whatever crime he committed. Should I come looking for you?"

Randy didn't want to admit it, but the chief's words made sense. This whole thing was giving him a headache. He ran his hands through his hair, clasped them behind his head, and looked up at the ceiling. "No." His answer sounded tired.

"I didn't think so." Nicolas stood and came around the desk. "Look, we both know that things are seldom as easy as we'd like them to be." He reached behind him and picked up a pad of paper. "Write down everything you can remember about your conversation with Liz Murphy. It's not an official statement, it's not something that is going to clear Maggie's name today, but it gives us a new angle to look at. Then do me a favor."

Randy took the offered pen and paper. "What?"

"Stay as far away from Liz Murphy as you can. Not just you, Maggie too. Let us do our job. Justice usually wins in the end."

His memory sizzled with distrust. Usually wasn't always.

The chief continued. "I know you think you're helping, but this is a police matter, and neither of you are trained investigators."

Randy latched onto the chief's words like a starving man presented with a slice of pizza. "So, you will be investigating?"

Nicolas held up a hand. "Let's just say we'll keep our eyes and ears open. If we find a reason to dig deeper into the life and times of Liz Murphy, we will."

Randy bent over the pad of paper and did as Nicolas had asked. Once he'd finished he stood and held out his hand. "Thanks, Nicolas, I appreciate your time."

Randy left the police station with mixed emotions. Encouraged that Nicolas believed him, but frustrated at the slow crawl of justice. He unlocked his car, slid behind the wheel, and stared out into space for a few seconds. He needed a moment to process before he picked up the kids and his attention fractured with their wants and needs.

Was there anything else he could do?

Randy pondered the question, turning over every nuance of his brief conversation with Maggie's friend and his meeting with Nicolas. He hated to answer no, but short of kidnapping Liz and hauling her to the police station, no was the only answer he had. At least he wasn't leaving completely empty-handed. Nicolas had promised extra ears and eyes on Liz until this thing was resolved. That had to be enough.

Father, please let that be enough. We both know Maggie

didn't do this. You can change hearts. You can open doors. You make all things new. I'm not telling You how to run Your business, but if You've got a plan, now would be a great time to share.

He reached for the ignition, started the car, and backed out of the parking spot. With a touch of the dashboard screen he connected the hands-free calling.

"Hey, Siri, call Grandma."

The mechanical voice was quick to answer. "Calling Grandma, mobile."

"Hello."

"Hey, Grandma. Are the kids ready?"

"Up and fed. We had waffles. They're dressed and waiting. We're finishing off the Christmas sugar cookies while we watch a movie."

Waffles and sugar cookies? Randy glanced at the time. It was barely ten. Max and Mariah were going to be on a sugar high they wouldn't come down from for hours. So much for his plan to work this afternoon.

Grandma Callie must have read his mind. "My house, my rules." She chuckled.

"Thanks, I think. Do me a favor. Put a lid on the cookie jar. I'll be there in ten minutes."

"Sure thing. I love you."

"Love you too. Bye."

Randy disconnected the call as another came through. He didn't recognize the number and figured it was probably spam. Since he didn't need an extended auto warranty, new health care coverage, or lower interest rates, he started to decline the call, but something made him hesitate.

"Hello."

"Is this Randy Caswell?"

The female voice that came through the car speakers had him gripping the steering wheel. "Yes."

"This is Liz Murphy. Can we talk?"

Randy took in his surroundings. This call needed his full attention. "Give me a second." He pulled into the Sonic parking lot, nosed into an empty stall, and put the car in park. "Go ahead."

"I just wanted you to know that I can't stop thinking about what you said this morning. I don't want Maggie to pay for my mistake. It's not fair to her or her kids."

Randy slumped in his seat as her words hit home, and part of the weight he'd been carrying around for the last week lifted from his shoulders. "Thank you, Liz. I appreciate that more than I can say. "

"I'm going to go to the cops like you asked, but I've got some things to work out first. There are some people I need to talk to, stuff I need to do."

He heard a sniff, and when she spoke again her voice was muffled, her words broken. "I just need a couple of days. I promise I'll get this all straightened out. Can you give me till Monday?"

Randy digested her words. "Monday works."

"Thank you. Could you let Maggie know we talked? After the way I treated her, she probably doesn't want to hear from me ever again. Tell her I'm sorry."

"Sure. I—"

Three quick beeps told him she'd hung up.

"Well, OK."

His hand hovered over the keypad. Who should he call first, Maggie or Nicolas? Neither, he decided. Telling Nicolas about the phone call would just sound like more interference on his part. Nicolas had been pretty clear about that. Besides, he'd have the whole story soon enough. As for Maggie... He'd pick up the kids, go get her, and treat them all to a celebration lunch.

Maggie was going to be free.

The thought made him sit straighter in the seat.

He'd been procrastinating over their plans for a week because he couldn't put his heart above his responsibilities. That wasn't an issue anymore. He could give her the ring, he could ask her the question that had been burning in his heart—and Max's—for days.

But how and where?

After everything they'd been through, he wanted to make the proposal something special and memorable. The restaurant at the top of the Devon Tower would have been the perfect setting, but they'd been there the night before.

Even if he could afford two meals like that in one week, it would seem like a rerun, flat and anticlimactic. No worries. He'd think of something. For right now, he'd just take a drive by Liz's house and make sure her car was still in the drive. He trusted Nicolas to do the right thing, but a little extra caution wouldn't hurt.

CHAPTER ELEVEN

A COLD JANUARY wind whistled through the alley as Maggie wrestled with the heavy back door to Crafted with Love bright and early Monday morning. She shifted the bulky box, balancing it with one hand underneath and her chin on top. She tugged the door until she was able to get a foot between it and the frame.

"I could use a little help here," she called, hoping someone in the break room would come to her aid. Her plea went unanswered, probably unheard, as the next gale-force gust blew her back a few inches, dislodging her foot as it threatened to carry her away. The door snapped shut with a mocking clank.

Maggie took a deep breath of the frigid air and winced as it chilled her throat and lungs. How could something so cold burn? Her gaze swept the alley. There were four other cars clustered around the door, so someone had to be inside the store. She braced to try again and jumped back as the door inched open.

Ember took one step out and braced her body against it, fighting against Mother Nature to keep it open long enough for Maggie to dash through. Once Maggie and the box cleared the opening, Ember hurried inside. They both jumped as the wind forced the door shut with a bang that rattled the building.

"I have never..." Ember's words trailed in disbelief.

"The weatherman said we'd have gusts up to seventy miles per hour today," Maggie said. "I think we have that plus some."

"Yeah." Ember studied Maggie. "Bless your heart, you must be frozen. Were you out there long?"

Maggie put the box on the table. "Seemed longer than it really was. Where is everyone?"

Ember waved to the main part of the store. "Ruthie needed some help situating a large piece she just finished."

"The hall tree?"

"How did you know?"

Maggie shrugged out of her coat, draped it across the back of a chair, and opened the box. "She was telling me about it before she left on the cruise. She said she'd intentionally held it back until after Christmas because her stuff was already taking up so much space."

"We're so understocked right now I'm almost glad she wait-ed," Ember said. "Someone will be really blessed to have that piece gracing their entry hall. It's hard to look at the finished product and see the beat-up hutch it used to be. I know it's meant to go in the hall for coats and stuff, but that padded bench just begs to be curled up on with a thick, fuzzy throw and a good book."

"I can't wait to see it." Maggie pulled a plastic container out of the box and removed the lid. The mini pecan pie muffins she'd baked early that morning filled the back room of the shop with the scents of brown sugar and baked nuts. As it mixed with the aroma of Ember's freshly brewed coffee, Maggie expected the rest of the group to gather without invitation.

Ember stared at the homemade treat with both hands over her slightly rounded belly. "Girlfriend, if we don't get you back to work soon, I'm going to be a whale. I don't know how something the size of a jelly bean can be hungry all the time, but this baby is already salivating." She plucked one of the muffins free, popped it into her mouth, and rolled her eyes heavenward." "Mmm...Mmm..."

"Hey, no fair." Holly came through the door and stopped with her hands on her hips. "I know there are two of you, but show some restraint." She passed the table on her way to the coffee pot and snagged a muffin for herself.

Sage followed. "That's your idea of restraint?"

"Yes," Holly answered. "You'll notice I'm making my coffee before I swallow this little piece of heaven whole."

Sage hip-bumped her sister out of the way and doctored her own drink. "Pig."

"Bully."

The words were barely out of their mouths before they bent toward each other and exchanged air kisses as the other crafters trouped in.

"Lacy, that quilt hanging from the coat hooks is the perfect homey touch," Ruthie said, "and Piper, the cross you arranged on the top shelf is pure genius. You have such an eye for color. If I didn't know better, I'd swear you'd been peeking into my workroom."

"No peeking, just inspired once you described it to us," Piper said. "Ember, take a look when you go back out. It looks amazing, but it needs some flowers."

"I'll see what I can do," Ember said.

Lacy nibbled at her treat. "Maybe we'll get lucky and sell the whole shebang."

"Wouldn't that be a great way to start the new year?" Maggie bit one of the pint-sized treats in half and studied Piper and Lacy from beneath her lashes while she chewed. She hadn't had the Christmas she'd longed for, but neither of her friends had either. Piper had lost the baby she carried almost three months before. Not having her kids close broke Maggie's heart, but at least she got to see them most days. They were alive and healthy. To lose a baby, full-term, like Piper had? That was almost more than Maggie could imagine. And if Lacy's recent moodiness was any indication, her second Christmas without her daughter hadn't been any easier than the first. Old grief or new. Both left a mark.

She swallowed, hoping that the good news she had to share would banish some of the shadows. These women had trusted her completely, had been so generous with their love and finances. Maggie couldn't wait to let them know that their loyalty hadn't been misplaced.

Today was the day this nonsense ended.

Today was the day Liz had promised to clear Maggie's name.

Today was the day Maggie's world went from out of control back to some sort of normal.

Giddy anticipation clogged the breath in her throat, but before she had a chance to open her mouth, Piper grabbed a second muffin.

"I've got to run. I'm already later than I wanted to be."

"Late?" Sage said. "It's barely seven-thirty."

Piper chewed and swallowed. Her eyelashes fluttered as she looked at Maggie. "Girl...mm!" After dusting crumbs from her fingers, she reached for her coat. "First day back after a long break is always hectic. I need to be in the office and available." She pulled her long hair free of the coat collar. "Ember, give me a call tonight if I miss anything important. See you guys later."

Maggie raised a finger. "I..."

A burst of cold air and a clank from the door, and Piper was gone.

Ruthie was already bundling up as well. "I've got to hustle

too." Her gaze lingered on the box of treats as she pulled the coat's zipper up to her neck. "Save me a couple of those, will you? I've got to be in the city for my yearly poke and prod in an hour. My doctor ordered fasting lab work. If I don't get out of here, not only will I be late but I'll give into temptation and blow my test results. Ditto what Piper said. Call me tonight if you need to." She was out the door before the chill of Piper's exit had dissipated.

Maggie slumped. So much for sharing her news with the group.

"What?" Lacy asked.

"What what?" Maggie responded.

"Please," Lacy said. "It's the first time I've seen a real smile on your face in a week. You're practically bouncing with excitement."

"You look like you're about to burst." Sage nudged a chair free and took a second one for herself. "Sit and spill."

Maggie did, waiting for the others to follow Sage's lead. Nervous energy had her popping back up almost immediately. "I can't sit. I'm a wreck." She took a gulp of air and blurted her news. "My friend is supposed to go talk to the cops today."

"What?" Holly said.

"Praise God," Ember whispered.

"How...?" Sage didn't finish. She just closed her eyes and released her own breath of relief.

"I'm so thankful you finally caught up with her," Lacy said. "More thankful that she's willing to do the right thing."

"Well, not so willing at first, but Randy got through to her." Maggie shared her encounter with Liz at the mall, Randy's initial failed attempt at persuasion, his conversation with Chief Black, and finally Liz's phone call and her plea for a little time.

"I've been a mess all weekend. Part of me just wants to go sit outside her house and make sure she doesn't change her mind.

But Randy promised Chief Black that we'd stay out of it. That's probably even more important now. I don't want her to feel pressured or do anything to make her change her mind." Maggie stretched her hands out over the table and watched as they trembled. "I can't stop shaking. I just want this to be over with. I've barely slept the last two nights. My house is spotless." She nodded at the muffins. "I've baked and frozen enough sweets that you guys won't eat them all in a month. I can't sit still long enough to bead or read."

She looked at Ember. "It sounds like Ruthie isn't available to work her shift today. Can I take her place? If I go home, I'll be crazy by noon. You don't even have to pay me."

Ember sent Maggie a sympathetic smile. "Of course you can. I think I can find something to keep your hands busy and your mind off the clock."

RANDY STROLLED around the perimeter of his classroom Monday morning, keeping a close eye on the twenty-four kids he called his own this year. Whispers and quiet giggles issued from some of the tables, a few muted sniffles from others. Most of the kids had returned to class with smiles and excited stories about what Santa had left under their trees. Two or three had clung to their mothers like it was the first day of school all over again.

But tears or laughter, this was Randy's domain, and after all the drama of the holiday break, he was happy to get back into his routine. Maybe that was the measure of a solid career choice, something that you truly missed when you were gone. He took a deep breath, allowing the familiar scents of paper, pencil shavings, and crayons to mingle in his lungs. It might not appeal to everyone, but it was sweet perfume to him.

"Mr. Caswell?"

Across the room, Lily Perkins was squirming in her seat and waving her arm frantically.

"Lily?"

She held up her coloring sheet. "I can't find my green. Is it OK if I make my grass purple?"

A loud snort sounded. "There's no such thing as purple grass. Girls are so silly." Scott Hampton, the class know-it-all, chimed in before Randy could answer.

Lily glared at Scott even as her lower lip trembled. "I am not silly. There is too purple grass. I had some in my Easter basket. You're just a meanie."

"That wasn't real grass, goofus."

"Mr. Caswell..."

Randy held up a hand as the rest of the kids stopped what they were doing and gave their attention to Lily and Scott. "OK, everyone, let's get back to work. Lily and Scott, join me at my desk, please."

The kids shuffled forward while Randy took his seat, crossed his arms, and drew in a deep breath.

Lily arrived first, her paper clutched in one hand, her eyes bright with tears.

Scott took his time. Randy had rules in his classroom, and Scott knew he'd broken one.

"I'm sorry," Lilly started, "I didn't mean to fight, but I can't find my green."

"No problem." Randy opened his desk drawer and pulled out a box of mixed and discarded crayons that he'd collected over the years. He lifted the lid and held it out to Lily. "Do you see what you need?"

The little girl pawed through the box and drew out a green crayon. "I'll bring it right back."

"You can keep it."

"Thanks." She started back to her seat.

"Wait right here for a second," Randy told her as Scott finally joined them. Randy gave the boy his full attention. "Do you know what you did wrong?"

"Yes, sir."

"Would you like it if someone called you silly or a goofus?"

Scott shook his head.

"Why?"

The little boy looked down at the scuffed toes of his shoes. "Because it's ugly, I guess."

"Exactly," Randy said. "Do you have something to say to Lily?"

The little boy clasped his hands behind his back with a jerky shrug. "Sorry," he mumbled.

"I think you can do better than that," Randy said. "And when you're talking to someone, you need to look at them and use their name."

Scott's sigh was beleaguered, but he lifted his head and faced Lily. "I'm sorry, Lily. I didn't mean to be mean."

He said the words so fast that it was hard to know where one stopped and the next started, but Lily obviously got it. She gave Scott a happy smile. "That's OK. Purple grass is sort of funny, I guess."

Before Randy could say anything else, the door to his classroom opened. His principal, Piper Goodson, stood in the doorway. Her normally pleasant expression appeared strained.

"Mr. Caswell, could I speak to you in the hall?"

"Sure. Give me a second." He looked down at Scott and Lily. "You two can go back to your seats." He stood. "Everyone else, keep working. I bought some new books over the break. We'll have story time when I've finished speaking to Ms. Goodson."

Randy joined Piper at the door. "What can I do for you?"

Piper jerked her head toward the other end of the hall, and Randy looked that direction.

Two uniformed cops stood next to the office door. Their hands rested on their guns, their stares rested on him.

"They asked me to come get you," Piper whispered. "What's going on?"

Randy was as confused as she was. "I don't have a clue. Did they say anything?"

"Something about a missing woman and you being the last one to speak to her."

Randy shifted as heat flooded his extremities.

Liz.

Had to be, but missing? Her car had been in the drive when he'd cruised by this morning.

She was supposed to turn herself in today.

One of the cops came toward them.

"Randy Caswell?"

"Yeah."

"We need you to come with us."

"Sure, just let me..." He motioned to his classroom.

"I'll take care of it," Piper told him. "Call me when you can."

"Yep," Randy answered as he walked to the main exit, the two cops on his heels.

CHAPTER TWELVE

"WHAT ARE YOU DOING?"

Poised with both hands wrapped around the vase of a new flower arrangement and one foot on the cushioned edge of Ruthie's new hall tree, Ember glanced over her shoulder at Maggie's question.

"I'm gonna—"

"No," Maggie said.

"But—"

"Get down this instant." Maggie put her fists on her hips. "Do you hate me?"

With both feet firmly on the floor, Ember faced Maggie with a frown. "Of course not."

"Do you hate Quinn?"

"Why would you—?"

"Because your climbing around on that thing, in your condition, is the fastest way to get rid of me and your husband. I'll be dead and buried and Quinn will be back in prison for my murder because I didn't stop you."

Ember giggled. "You goof."

"Maybe, but there's no way you're getting up there." Maggie held out her hands. "Give that to me."

Ember held out the flowers but pulled them back before Maggie could take them. "Why don't you get up there first? That way you can get your balance before your hands are full."

Maggie rolled her eyes. "That's really good advice. Maybe you should remember it." She took off her shoes and climbed onto the padded bench. Just as she twisted a bit to grab ahold of the heavy vase, her phone rang.

The women stared at each other over the blue and yellow silk pansies for a second before Maggie scrambled back to the floor.

She'd been waiting for the phone to ring all morning. Now that it did, her heart threatened to pound right out of her chest. "It has to be—"

"Well, answer it," Ember said.

Maggie swiped the call open without even looking at the screen. "Hello."

"I hope you're happy."

The words were so far removed from what Maggie'd expected that it took her a moment to put them together with the voice. "Sophie?"

"They just arrested my son. This is your fault."

Maggie's knees went weak and she sank down to the bench. "What? How could they...? Why?"

"How should I know." Sophie's voice grew shriller with each word. "Karla called Mom, Mom called me. She didn't have any details, but I can guess at some of them. This has your despicable fingerprints all over it."

"This has to be a misunderstanding," Maggie said. "I'll go over there right now—"

"Haven't you done enough? Why can't you just own up to what you did and take your punishment like a woman? Get out of my son's life and leave those babies to a family who'll give them the sort of life they deserve. Haven't you figured out that you're just a means to an end?"

"What?"

"Do I have to spell it out for you? Randy could never love someone like you. He just wants Max and Mariah. If you were any kind of a mother, you'd get out of the way and let them get on with their lives."

The phone went dead in Maggie's hand. She didn't look up until a tear plopped onto the screen.

Ember sat next to her and put an arm around her shoulders. "What was that all about?"

"That was Randy's mom." She swiped at the moisture under her eyes. "She said they arrested Randy."

"Why...?"

"All I know is what Sophie said. I don't know what to do. I thought today was the day things would get better, instead... everything's just more messed up."

"Look at me," Ember said. When Maggie raised her eyes, Ember continued. "Did you do this? Were those your drugs in the car?"

"No. Oh, Ember, no. I'd never..." Maggie's words were punctuated with sobs.

"I didn't think so. Wait here for just a second."

Ember disappeared into the back room.

Randy arrested? How could things have gotten so twisted?

Ember came back in and sat next to Maggie, patting the Bible she had with her. "I want to share a verse with you." She paused as if waiting for permission. When Maggie remained silent, Ember opened the Bible and flipped a few pages. "Here we are. 'Be strong and of a good courage, fear not, nor be afraid of them: For the Lord thy God, He it is that doth go with thee: He will not fail thee, nor forsake thee.'"

Ember closed the book and looked at Maggie. "Moses gave that advice to Joshua when he was getting ready to face the biggest battle of his life. I think you and Joshua are a lot alike."

"How do you mean?"

"You've both fought really hard to get to this point in your life. You're both facing a big, scary battle that isn't going to go away. You both have a promise. God swore that Joshua would enter the Promised Land victorious." Ember studied Maggie for a second. "Do you have a promise, Maggie?"

"I thought I did. But, I've been a screw-up all my life. Maybe I got that wrong too."

"I don't know about that. But I do know about fighting for what's important. Those babies and the future you want with them and Randy... If you don't fight this battle, who will? Sophie?"

Ember's suggestion washed over Maggie like hot lava. "Over my dead body."

"Then, girlfriend, put on your shoes, dry your tears, and get over to the police station. Fight for what belongs to you. Sophie might be an intimidating enemy, but you don't need to be afraid of her. God's got your back. He's not going to let you down."

RANDY WATCHED Nicolas Black pace the small interrogation room. The man's expression was intimidating, but Randy'd known Nicolas his whole life. He wasn't intimidated. What did bother him, more than a little, was the quiet presence of an unknown officer studying him from the corner of the room and the tiny device in the middle of the table, which was obviously recording their every word.

"So, you're telling me that you spoke to Liz Murphy after I expressly told you to stay out of it?"

"She called me."

"And I'm just hearing this because...?"

"Because I'd just left your office. You'd just told me that anything Liz said to me wasn't going to make a difference. What was I supposed to do? You'd already promised to keep an eye on things. Why bother barging back into your office to share something else you couldn't use? I left it in your hands, just like you asked."

Chief Black sat in the chair opposite Randy and ran his hands through his graying hair. "All right. Take me through everything you've done since you left here Friday."

Randy crossed his arms and leaned on the table. "Not until you tell me what's going on. Why exactly you thought it was necessary to send a couple of cops to haul me out of school like some sort of ax murderer when a simple phone call would have accomplished the same thing?" He glanced at the stranger in the corner. "I mean, really? You've known me my whole life."

Nicolas matched his pose. "Our relationship is why I sent the cops and why we will have an unbiased witness to everything that happens from this point forward. This investigation needs to be pristine. Now I need you to answer my questions. If I like what I hear, I'll be as forthcoming as I can be."

It wasn't the answer Randy wanted, but it was all he was likely to get. "After I left your office Friday, I called Grandma to let her know I was on the way to pick up the kids. I was headed there when Liz called me." He related the contents of that conversation as best as he remembered. "I'd pulled into the Sonic to take the call, and when she hung up, I decided to get a drink and take Grandma a milkshake as a thank-you. I used my debit card to pay for the order." It was difficult to keep the sarcasm out of his voice when he added, "You can check my bank records to verify that if you need to."

"Count on it," the chief answered. His voice was missing any hint of amusement. "Continue."

"I picked the kids up."

"What time?"

"Probably around eleven-thirty. From there I drove to Maggie's. Liz's promise to come clean to you gave us something to celebrate. We had lunch at Mama Rosita's. Do you need to know what everyone ordered?"

Nicolas sighed. "What I need is for you to take this seriously, for your sake and everyone else's. After lunch?"

"I took Maggie home. We visited for a couple of hours while the kids played with some of the toys that Maggie keeps over there, and then the kids and I went home."

"Did you leave the house again that evening?"

Randy struggled to keep the impatience out of his voice. "No, not until church yesterday morning. Today was the first day back at school. I had some preparation to do that took most of Friday evening and Saturday. Maggie came over to the house about noon on Saturday to occupy the kids so I could work. She fixed dinner, got Max and Mariah settled in for the night, and left about nine. If I remember correctly, I shook your hand after both services Sunday. I was at the school bright and early this morning, and here we are."

They ran through the story a half dozen more times with Nicolas peppering Randy with old questions phrased in new ways. Randy's version never varied. He finally leaned back in his chair and crossed his arms. "Look, you have everything I can tell you. Will you please tell me what's going on?"

"We got a call from Liz Murphey's next-door neighbor early this morning," Nicolas said. "He'd gone out to get his paper and noticed the front door to Ms. Murphy's house was open. He thought that was a little odd since her car was in the driveway. In an effort to be a good neighbor, he went to check on her. He called her name several times, and when he didn't get a response, he entered the house, worried that she might be sick or something. He didn't find her, but since the house looked, in his words, 'tossed,' he called us.

"We didn't find her, but we found her phone." His expression turned suspicious. "The last call she made was to your number. Are you sure you had no contact with her after she called you?"

"I haven't talked to her."

Nicolas stared at him and Randy began to sweat. That look would have broken Al Capone. "That's a pretty flimsy answer."

Randy met his gaze and tried not to squirm in his seat. His conscience finally got the better of him. "I drove by her house a couple of times." The words were a mumbled admission. "But I think you already know that."

"Our nosy neighbor described a car he'd noticed a few times over the weekend. Blue, four-door Buick Regal. Sound familiar?"

Randy didn't say anything.

"You lied to me."

"No. I did just as I told you. I just used the times I was out to keep an eye on the situation."

Chief Black pinched the bridge of his nose. "After everything I told you, you just couldn't leave it alone, could you?"

"I couldn't just sit around and do nothing. I didn't think that making sure she stuck close to home was in violation of your request."

"Except she's missing, and your actions make you look guilty."

"You know I'd never..." Randy let his words trail. "Can we just get back to the positive? She's gone but that just proves our point, right?"

"How do you figure?"

"Well..." Randy paused to organize his thoughts. "If she ran, that's evidence of guilt, isn't it? You have to investigate now, and you have access to her home. You can search for evidence of drugs, you can take fingerprints. There has to be something there that will clear Maggie's name. All you have to do is find it."

The look Nicolas gave Randy had him squirming like a bug under a microscope.

"I mean, it's obvious that she ran. That whole story about needing a couple of days...? Come on. She probably had her boyfriend take her someplace."

"Well, we can't know that for sure since you neglected to share that info in a timely manner." Nicolas reached over to turn off the recorder.

"Let me tell you how this works. We have the house cordoned off as a crime scene. We will be searching and printing, but OSBI is just coming off the holidays. Any prints we send to them, in the absence of obvious foul play, are going to go to the bottom of a very tall pile. What would normally take a couple of days is likely to take a week or more. That's the bad news. The good news is that, since we have new threads to pull, I'm going to call the DA and recommend he put a hold on Maggie's case until we can see what's what."

"Nicolas, that's great news. I really..."

The chief held up a hand. "It's a pause, not a dismissal. I'm going to tell you again. Stay out of this. I know you have your reasons for wanting to stay on top of this but you need to trust the system and let us do our jobs. If you, or Maggie, hear from Liz Murphy, I need to know immediately."

"So I'm free to go?"

"Driving by her house wasn't the smartest thing you ever did, but I can't arrest you for being stupid. I'll call the school and talk to your boss and explain why I had to pull you out of there.

But..." he paused and pinned Randy with a steely gaze. "If I catch you anywhere near that house...if I find out you had contact with her and didn't tell me immediately. I'll lock you up and throw away the key. Now get out of here."

Randy hurried out of the room and into the front of the station. He was startled when Maggie leapt from a chair and ran into his arms.

"Whoa! What are you...?"

"Your mom said they arrested you." Maggie lifted her tear-stained face to his. "I'm so sorry."

Arrested? Randy pulled her close and kissed her forehead. "That's just Mom's histrionics. They just had some questions about Liz."

"Liz? Is she here? Did she keep her promise?"

The expectation on Maggie's face almost broke Randy's heart. He wasn't sure if everything he'd been told was good or bad, but he needed someplace more private either way. "Let's get out of here. I've got news."

CHAPTER THIRTEEN

Randy put the book away and tucked the blanket up around Max's chin. He stirred slightly. "I love you, Dad." The words were a sleepy mumble.

"I love you, too, buddy," Randy whispered. "I'll see you in the morning." He paused in the doorway before turning out the light, watching the blanket rise and fall with Max's breathing, and asked himself for the millionth time how it was possible to love another man's child so deeply. He didn't really need an answer. If ever a little boy had been made just for him, it was Max.

Thanks, Father.

He pulled the door closed and stopped to listen outside Mariah's room. Not a peep.

His shoulders slumped as the last twelve hours caught up with him.

What a day.

And it wasn't quite over. Randy moved through the quiet house, picking up the detritus of a busy family. Yes, it was tedious and monotonous but, despite what his unencumbered, single friends might think, it was fulfilling at the same time. This was the life he'd wanted for himself. He knew it was the one Maggie wanted as well. He couldn't wait until these end-of-day chores could be shared with her, every night, for the rest of their lives."

He gathered Max's homework into a neat pile, putting it in the boy's backpack for the next day. A glimpse of something purple had him stooping to look under the edge of the sofa. Mariah's missing tennis shoe was his reward. A quick trip back down the hall reunited it with its mate. At least he wouldn't spend thirty minutes looking for it in the morning.

He finished loading the dishwasher, added a soap pod, and used the delayed start feature to set it to run after midnight. He needed a long hot shower to wash away the tension of the day, and he wasn't willing to share the hot water with the dinner dishes.

The morning was a surreal memory. But Randy held tightly to the positive aspects of the day. With the police seriously looking at Liz Murphy, it was just a matter of time before the truth came out and Maggie was officially cleared of the charges against her.

Some might call that wishful thinking, but if he didn't have hope, he had nothing.

Once the charges were dropped, they could get on with their lives and, thanks to a couple of articles he'd read after dinner, he knew just how the next steps would play out. His idea needed a little refinement and a whole lot of meteorological cooperation, but one way or another, he'd have a ring on Maggie's finger before the weekend.

The thought loosened something in his chest and gave him space to breathe. He and Maggie'd spent a lot of time together over the last year and a half. They were on the same page when it came to their future. A short engagement, an intimate spring wedding to accommodate his teaching schedule, an adoption to make Max and Mariah truly his, and two more babies to complete their family.

Mariah would be two in a few months, and even though Randy intended to give the sibling project his full attention, there was no getting around the fact that she'd likely be three or more before they could make her a big sister. She mothered her baby dolls with such tenderness, Randy couldn't wait to see how she handled the real thing.

Another girl first, he mused. That way, the two girls could grow up being best friends with a strong, loving brother on each end, sort of like protective bookends.

He liked that picture a lot.

His phone rang and shook him out of his pleasant daydream.

He glanced at the screen. Samantha Archer. Family friend and the social worker assigned to Max and Mariah's case.

Business or pleasure?

A niggle of dread tugged at his gut as a second ring filled the silence.

Dread?

He was just being paranoid. Who could blame him after the last couple of weeks?

He swiped the call open.

"Hey, Sam, what's up?"

"Funny. I was just about to ask you the same question."

Randy swallowed as the niggle of dread became a lump of lead. The voice on the other end of the phone didn't sound like his longtime family friend but the no-nonsense social worker.

The dynamics and relationships were complicated. His grandma Callie's best friend was Karla McAlister. Nicolas was

Karla's son. Samantha was married to Nicolas's stepson, Patrick. What that all boiled down to was that there were no secrets in the group, which led to the potential for a lot of trouble. He leaned against the kitchen counter and ran his free hand through his hair.

"Are you there?" Samantha's tone bordered on chilly.

"Sort of late for a business call, isn't it?"

"Depends on your point of view. I just got home from dinner with my in-laws. When I heard that one of my foster parents spent the morning at the police station being questioned about a crime, that bothered me. When I discovered that crime is closely related to an ongoing investigation involving one of my cases, a case, I might add, that no one thought it important enough to notify me about, that gets my attention. When the foster father in the first scenario is romantically involved with the birth mother in the second... Well let's just say that deserves a phone call. Don't you think?"

It was impossible for Randy to miss the mixture of sarcasm and frustration in Samantha's voice.

"I should have called, but it all came to nothing and frankly, I didn't think it was important."

"Randy, when it comes to those kids, everything is important." Her sigh filled his ear. "What I find most disturbing... what I can't quite wrap my brain around is the fact that this has been going on for nearly two weeks and neither of you called me. When were you planning to tell me, after Maggie was sentenced?" The censure in her tone was unmistakable.

Randy hurried to do some damage control. "That's not going to happen. She didn't do anything wrong and neither did I. This whole mess is about to blow over, and we can all get on with our lives."

"I wish it were that easy," Samantha said. "But it isn't. I

want you to know that if it were anyone else, I'd be picking kids up right now."

Her words were the sucker punch that He'd lived in fear of. "Don't—"

"Then you need to listen to me. You've done an amazing job with Max and Mariah. There aren't a lot of single young men who would take on this kind of job and flourish like you have.

"I'm not gonna lie. I had some reservations about the situation between you and Maggie in the beginning. My agency's job is to see that the children in our care have safe, loving homes to live in. You and Maggie have taken that to a whole new level. But as nice as that is, it poses some unique problems."

"Like?" Randy asked.

"After the last two weeks you have the audacity to ask me that?"

"It's on the verge of being history. I'd think you'd be pleased and relieved."

Samantha's heavy sigh echoed in Randy's ear. "None of that has any bearing on my part in this. Max and Mariah are my only responsibility. Of course I want Maggie's name cleared. She's worked every step of her service plan with the kind of diligence that I don't get to see very often. I know she was looking forward to completing the program and getting her kids back next week." She paused, her next words a whisper. "I just don't see that happening, next week or next month."

Randy groped for a kitchen chair as Samantha's words threatened to drop him to his knees. "What do you mean?"

"I've got a mother with a history of neglect involved in an ongoing drug investigation. And now the woman she says is responsible is missing under mysterious circumstances and you're a suspect. We all need to take a step back until we get this mess sorted out. I need to know if I can depend on you to put the kids ahead of your heart."

"Sam, please. This will kill Maggie."

"I'm sorrier about that than you can imagine. Can I count on you?"

"To do what exactly?"

"I'm offering you the chance to keep Max and Mariah in your care—"

"Absolutely."

"While restricting Maggie's access and your contact with each other."

Her words sucked the air out of his lungs.

"Hopefully, it'll just be temporary. We can revisit the state of the service plan once all of this is behind us. But as much as we're hoping for the best, we need to be prepared for the worst."

"Worst how?" His words sounded loud and harsh in the quiet house.

"I need you to calm down," Sam said. "I'm pulling for Maggie. I am, but if they don't find this woman and this thing goes to court with Maggie as the defendant, then nothing you or I want is going to make any difference. It's going to be in the hands of the DA at that point, and our DA takes a hard line on drug cases, especially opioids."

"But if she's innocent—"

"We both want to believe that, but once they delve into Maggie's past, they're going to find a woman who had her children removed from her home due to neglect and *suspected* drug use."

"She wasn't charged with a crime," Randy argued. "Every single drug test you guys have required has come back negative."

"And for that, I'll thank God and pray that those results can be used in her favor. But that doesn't change the fact that she's in the system. They'll find the details and they'll use them." Samantha's voice was tired when she continued. "Trust me, I can sympathize with her predicament. You know my story. I understand about being a young mother trying to keep a family afloat. But the district attorney won't care about any of that. It's an election year, and he's promised to crack down on the opioid problem. If he takes this to court, he'll do everything he can to make sure Maggie serves time. With the way the evidence stacks up now, he'll likely succeed."

"How much time?"

"The maximum is twelve months in county jail, but it's not about jail time."

"What do you mean?"

"Everything changes if she goes to jail. She has no criminal record now, but she will then. She won't be able to do the job she's trained to do. She'll have issues finding housing with a record. She'll have to complete a new service plan with us once she's released."

Randy closed his eyes at the picture Sam was painting. *Dear God, please don't let this happen. Maggie doesn't deserve any of this.* He swallowed. "Give me worst case."

"Between crowded court dockets, a maximum twelve-month sentence, a new eighteen-month service plan with us, one with stricter guidelines than you've had before..."

Randy held his breath. This couldn't be happening. In what sort of world did an innocent woman lose everything?

"You could be looking at another three years before Maggie has a chance at getting her kids back."

Sam didn't speak for several seconds. Maybe she was giving him the chance to absorb what she'd told him. It didn't matter. Her next words only made things worse.

"I know your first inclination is going to be to call Maggie when we get off the phone. I'm asking you not to."

"But—"

"In fact, as Max and Mariah's caseworker, I have to insist that you don't. I need to be the one discussing this with her. And I think, until this gets worked out, it's in everyone's best interest if I am your contact point. We also need to go back to a more structured visitation schedule."

"*Everyone's* best interest? I think Maggie would disagree with that. I certainly do."

"Max and Mariah's best interest then. As much as I love you, as much as I like Maggie, those kids are my first priority."

Silence stretched between them.

Sam broke it. "This isn't a request, Randy. I need your word or I'll have to come get the kids."

Randy bowed his head over the table. Not giving Maggie a heads-up on what was coming felt like the worst possible betrayal. Not giving Sam his word forced her into a decision he wasn't prepared to live with. A sick feeling washed over him. It would be Tait all over again. Randy's fault all over again.

His words were weary when he finally responded. "I won't tell her anything. And I won't let her see the kids. What about visitation?"

"I'll get back with you tomorrow about our next steps."

Randy sat at the table for a long time after Sam hung up. He was numb. His fingers itched to call Maggie, but he couldn't. He tried to pray, but he couldn't seem to do that, either. He wanted to crawl into bed, pull the covers over his head, and stay there until this was over.

But that wasn't an option.

Three more years? The added time with the kids didn't bother him. He wanted Max and Mariah forever. But it would kill Maggie.

There had to be a way to make this better. Maybe his mother had been right about the whole adoption thing. Not for the snarky reasons she'd outlined of course. But if he could adopt the kids, they'd be safe from the threat of being put in a strange home. If he adopted them now, Maggie's time away from them would be cut in half. He knew those drugs weren't hers, and if the kids were legally his, he and Maggie could get married just as soon as she served her time. That would eliminate her need to spend another eighteen months on a new service plan.

And his concern wasn't just for Maggie. Max would be devastated if his mom went to jail. Maybe he could take the kids on a vacation to give them something else to focus on.

Randy ran his hands through his hair as the realities of what he needed to do stacked on top of each other like a Lego castle built by a mad scientist. Adoption...vacations...an extended period of time without the woman he loved. None of this was going to be an easy sell where Maggie was concerned, but he had to be prepared to try.

He'd ripped up the papers his mother had given him, but he had a computer. He could find the information he needed.

Searching for vacation info for three was tedious but doable. Randy salved his heart with the knowledge that three could be changed to four easily enough.

The adoption forms were another story.

He read the forms as they came off the printer and felt like a traitor. His stomach filled with bile as he filled in some of the blanks. By the time he got to the portion that discussed grounds for the petition, he was so angry that the plastic barrel of the pen snapped in his fingers. Even if Maggie agreed, he couldn't do this. He couldn't ask Maggie to give up her rights. What happened when she got out of jail? Would she have to adopt her own kids once they were married? The whole thing was insane.

Maybe he should just propose and get it over with. Then if the worst happened the kids would be legally his. But that didn't feel right either. He didn't want anyone to see his marriage to Maggie as a last ditch convenience.

"God, tell me what to do."

Trust Me son, I have a plan.

Those words should have comforted him. They didn't. He gathered up the papers and tapped them into a stack.

His brain was numb.

Maybe there would be answers tomorrow.

MAGGIE SANK into a chair and stared at the phone Monday night. A sick rage boiled up inside of her as the conversation she'd just had with Max and Mariah's caseworker replayed in her head.

A return to scheduled visitation.

No unauthorized contact with Randy.

A possible year of jail time.

Another service plan to work through once she got out.

No.

No.

No.

"NO!"

An agonized scream clawed at her throat, begging for freedom. Instead, she drew her arm back and launched the phone at the far wall with all of her strength. The phone missed the wall and landed, unharmed, on the sofa cushions. Her aim was as good as everything else in her life right now.

She wrapped her arms around herself and huddled into a ball. How could this be happening? She'd done everything that CPS had required of her. She'd listened to every little whisper God put into her heart. But she was still going to lose the most important people in her life if something didn't change. Soon.

I have a plan, Daughter. A path for your feet and a future you can't begin to imagine.

Maggie looked up when the gentle words resonated in her heart. Tears filled her eyes. It was hard not to draw comfort from the promise contained in those words. It was equally hard not to scoff, just a little. She could imagine a whole lot, and none of it would resemble the misery Samantha Archer had just outlined.

Shame at her sarcastic thoughts poked at her conscience and she bowed her head. She started to apologize, but the words froze on her lips. Why bother? God knew her every thought and motivation. What good was saying sorry when she was still angry?

Maggie slipped to her knees by the chair and buried her head in the cushion. She might as well be honest and see what happened. "I don't know what You want me to do. You made me a promise, and I've done everything I know to do to get there. I thought things were finally turning around. I was so excited. Now things are worse, which I hadn't even thought possible." An emotion she didn't have a name for threatened to shred her heart, and she couldn't breathe. Her insides felt like they were coming apart. She clutched the cushion to keep from screaming. When she had control of her voice, her words came out in a frantic, gasping plea. "Father, please don't take my babies away from me. They're everything I have. I can't live without them." The rest of what she wanted to say dissolved into weeping.

Be calm, child, and trust Me.

This time she didn't scoff. Maggie pulled the gentle words around her like a heated throw on a cold day and allowed the promise they contained to rebuild her peace and her hope. "I do trust You, Father." Her heart lightened as she realized how much she meant it.

Be still and know that I am God.

Not the voice in her heart this time, but the echo of a Bible verse from a Sunday School lesson several weeks before.

Maggie crawled across the room, dug her phone out of the couch, and googled the verse. With every bit of commentary she read, that cloak of peace settled more firmly on her shoulders. The verse was about more than just sitting quietly and listening for God. It was a reminder that God fought for her when she couldn't fight for herself.

What she saw in the words spoke to her on a completely different level than they ever had before. There were battles she was never meant to fight. During those times, times like now, she was to take a step back and let God do what He did best. Her job was to watch from the sidelines and be amazed at His unfailing goodness.

She buried her face in her hands. "What You're asking me to do is the hardest thing I've ever done," she whispered. "How can I not claw and fight for my kids and my future with everything I have inside me? I do trust You, but to do nothing seems so wrong, almost ungrateful. They're my babies. I love them too much to get this wrong."

The response that filled her heart held warmth and the barest hint of a smile. *You are my daughter. I love you too much to get this wrong.*

Maggie looked up as if searching for the source of the words. She lifted her face and her hands and wept as her Father's quiet assurance washed over her. Somewhere in the process, God's simple promise worked its way into her heart and brought a peace she shouldn't have felt. Nothing had changed. Liz was still missing, and without her, Maggie was still going to bear the blame for those drugs. When she woke up tomorrow, she wouldn't have the luxury of seeing her babies whenever she wanted.

But, it was as if there was bubble wrap around her heart,

some invisible something that shielded her and brought her peace. When the tears were spent, she stretched out on the couch in exhaustion and knew beyond a doubt that she was held by the strongest hands in the universe.

Her whispered, "Thank You, Father," was the last thing she remembered before her mind drifted away in the first uninterrupted night's sleep in nearly two weeks.

CHAPTER FOURTEEN

MAGGIE WOKE up to light streaming through her window and a strange buzzing sound. She opened her eyes, momentarily confused about what she was doing on the couch. Memories from the night before flooded her mind, and she braced for an onslaught of pain, but the bubble wrap was still in place. Her Father had made her a promise and she could, she *would*, trust Him, even if it didn't make sense.

She wrapped one of the throw pillows in her arms and closed her eyes. "Good morning, Father. Thank You for rest. Thank You for peace. Howg do people survive without You?"

Her whispered question was answered by more buzzing.

Maggie sat up and tried to locate the source, but it vanished as quickly as it started. She stood, stretched, and was trying to decide which she needed more, fresh coffee or clean clothes, when the buzzing returned.

Was that her phone? Where had she left it? When the noise came a fourth time, Maggie realized it was coming from the couch. She crouched down, tossed cushions and pillows aside, and finally found the device wedged in a crevice where it must have settled sometime in the night. The phone buzzed a fifth time as she looked at the screen. The only notifications she saw were in Facebook messenger. She swiped the app open but didn't see anything new from any of her friends.

But someone was really trying to reach her. An overwhelming certainty that it was important had Maggie rushing to her laptop. Sometimes, a girl needed to see more than what the phone could offer.

When the computer booted up, Maggie opened Messenger and found the message requests. Her heart jumped when she read the name on the notifications. Five messages, in quick succession, from Dianne Murphy awaited her response. She read through them in breathless anticipation.

Maggie, I need to talk to you.

This is Liz's sister, Dianne. I got your name off Liz's friend list.

Have you heard from Liz since Christmas?

Please answer me, it's important.

This isn't a scam. If you don't want to talk to me here, please call me.

Maggie's hands shook as she scooped up her phone and punched in the number included at the end of the last message. It didn't even have time to complete a full ring before it was answered by a weary voice.

"Maggie Hart?"

"Yes."

"Thank God. I was afraid you wouldn't call me."

And she probably shouldn't have. Especially given Chief Black's orders to stay out of the investigation, but this had to be an answer to last night's prayer, and there was no way Maggie was walking away from it. "You're Liz's sister?"

"Yes. Have you talked to her lately?" Dianne hurried on as if she were afraid Maggie might hang up before she had a chance to explain. "Liz came to visit me a few days before Christmas.

She said that you loaned her your car. I haven't heard from her since, and I'm worried. Have you talked to her?"

Maggie chewed her lip, wondering how to answer that question.

"She brought your car back, right?"

What an odd thing to ask. "Yeah."

A heavy sigh echoed through the phone. "Thank God."

Maggie didn't miss the relief laced through those words. "Look, I can tell you're worried. I've got my own problems with Liz right now. Maybe if you start at the beginning, we can help each other." The silence that followed her suggestion was so long that Maggie pulled the phone away from her ear for a second to make sure that the connection was still good.

"Liz is my baby sister," Dianne began. "I'm twelve years older. She was just a kid when I left home to go to college. We've never been super close, and she's had some...issues, but even with that, I never thought she'd steal from me."

Something jerked to attention in Maggie's spirit. "She stole from you?"

"I think so. I hurt my back on the job a few weeks ago. I've been living on pain pills while the doctors and my insurance hashed out the best course of treatment. They finally decided on surgery right before Christmas. Between my doctor and the surgeon, I pretty much had a pharmacy in my medicine cabinet. I don't like pills. I've seen the damage they can do first hand, so I've been careful to take as few as I could get away with. I finished the bottle on my bedside table this morning. When I went to the bathroom to get a spare bottle, they were all gone. It breaks my heart to think that Liz took them, but she's the only person who's been here."

Maggie put the phone on speaker and lowered her head into her hands. *Please, Father, let her be willing to help me.*

Dianne's voice was tired when she continued. "She has a

history of addiction, and when I discovered the missing pills, my inability to reach her had me really worried. I was afraid she'd gotten high and put your car into a ditch or something. I wanted to make sure she hadn't killed herself between here and there."

Maggie looked up and wiped tears of relief from her eyes. "She was healthy as of last weekend."

"So you've talked to her?"

"Seen her, talked to her. I can give you her new number if you like, but the police have her phone, so I don't think it will do you much good."

"I'd like...wait, the police? Why do the police have her phone?"

Maggie filled Dianne in on the whole story, beginning with the Christmas Eve traffic stop and ending with the social worker's call the night before. "Look, Liz is your sister, and you don't know me, but I really need your help." She closed her eyes and sent up a silent prayer. "Is there any way that you'd be willing to come to Garfield and tell the police what you told me...what you suspect and why? At the risk of sounding overly dramatic, my whole life depends on it."

"You poor, sweet girl," Dianne said. "Of course I'll help. You did a favor for a friend, and look what you've received in return. I'm just sorry my sister put you through all this grief. I'm sorry I was too distracted when she visited to notice that she'd fallen back into her old habits. This could actually be an answer to my prayer. Maybe the authorities can get her the help she needs. Heaven knows my parents and I haven't been able to."

"Can you come today?" Maggie asked.

"I can't drive just yet, but I have a friend on the police force here in Tulsa. He knows our family and has some experience with Liz's history. Let me see if I can reach him. Maybe he can come to me, take my statement, and contact the police in Garfield."

Relief threatened to melt every bone in Maggie's body as days of uncertainty and tension loosened. There were fresh tears, but this time they were mixed with hope. "Thank you. Thank God! You don't have any idea..."

"Oh, I think I do. You hold tight. We're going to get you out of this mess."

Maggie held the phone for a long time after the call was disconnected. She was weak with relief, but there was an odd energy buzzing through her at the same time. First things first.

"Thank You, Father. I'm so sorry I doubted You. You just handed my life back to me. I've taken a lot for granted over the years. Never, ever let me forget how close I came to losing everything and how You rescued me." She looked heavenward as tears streamed down her cheeks. "I was never alone. I was never abandoned. Thank You so much." Maggie took a deep breath and straightened. "Touch Dianne. Bring her healing. Speak to Liz wherever she is. I'm not happy with her, but I forgive her. She needs help. Make a way for her to get it."

The next few hours seemed like a lifetime as Maggie struggled to keep her hands busy and her mind off the passing time. Little niggles of worry tried to gain a foothold, but she used prayer to banish them as quickly as they appeared. The fact that Dianne didn't call her back caused a few anxious moments, but Maggie refused to give in to doubt.

She wanted to call Dianne back to see what was happening, wanted to share what she'd learned with Randy, wanted to plead her innocence one more time with her caseworker or Chief Black. She did none of those things. Instead every time the itch of anxiety surfaced, she whispered Psalm 46:10. "Be still and know that I am God."

By midafternoon, every corner of her house sparkled after hours of elbow grease. There were fresh cookies on the counter because, God willing, the end was in sight and she would see her kids tonight. A selection of new jewelry awaited her next trip to the store. She wasn't surprised to find that she couldn't nap, couldn't read, couldn't watch TV. The waiting was going to kill her.

She was just setting up the ironing board to press her scrubs for her anticipated return to work on Monday when her doorbell rang. Maggie pulled the door open to find Garfield's Chief of Police standing on her porch with his hat in his hands. She wrapped her arms around herself, not sure if she should be relieved or frightened.

"Chief Black."

"Ms. Hart. May I come in?"

The polite request bolstered Maggie's courage. She moved out of the doorway and motioned to the living room. "Have a seat."

The burly cop eased himself into a chair. "You have a nice little place here."

Maggie looked around the room, trying to see it through the eyes of a stranger. He was right. The house was one of those taken-for-granted blessings, tidy and warm. Not too big but not too small. Hardwood floors with large area rugs to keep the chill off bare feet. She'd decorated the living room in shades of gray and yellow, and the large windows let in lots of natural light.

But with all of that, the whole place seemed to be waiting for the kids who would add laughter, life, and the chaos of family to the space. "Thanks. I moved in a couple of months ago in preparation." She swallowed back tears. "In preparation for getting my kids back. They're supposed to come home next week."

The chief nodded. "Let's see if we can get that back on track."

Maggie lowered herself to the sofa, afraid to speak for fear of jinxing what she hoped he was about to say.

"I've had a busy day, highlighted by a visit from a detective from the Tulsa police department. Nice guy. He gave me a written statement from Dianne Murphy and provided some personal insight about your friend Liz."

Maggie's heart pounded. Her fingers were pressed over her mouth. A silent prayer repeated in her mind.

"While I was speaking to Detective Holman, I got an interesting report back from OSBI. The prints on the bag of pills we found in your car didn't match yours. They match the prints we've gathered from Liz Murphy's house." He leaned forward and turned the brim of his hat in his hands. "You've been through a lot, and I know what this whole thing could have cost you. I wanted to come by and tell you, in person, that all the charges against you have been dropped."

Maggie leaned forward, barely able to hold herself upright as all of her joints went limp with relief.

It was over.

There was no way to stop the tears that shook her as she took it all in.

The chief was by her side in an instant, a hesitant hand on her back. "Please don't do that. If Randy finds out I made you cry again, I'll have to put him in jail until he cools off."

Maggie looked up and smiled through her tears. "Chief, you can make me cry every day of the week as long as the news you bring me is as wonderful as this."

CHAPTER FIFTEEN

RANDY BUCKLED Mariah into her car seat in the back of his grandma's car after school on Thursday. He went around to the other side and helped Max get settled. There was a light in the little boy's eyes that had been missing for days.

"Good luck," Max whispered. "Be sure to tell her how pretty she is. I know it's gross"—he wrinkled his nose—"but the women on TV like that kind of thing."

Randy ruffled his hair. "You let me worry about that."

"I love you, Dad."

"I love you too, buddy." He straightened and looked at the kids nestled in the back seat. It was hard to remember his life and his routines before they came into it. There was no way he'd trade what he had now for a return to those things. With a wink at Max, he closed the door and looked over the top of the car to where Grandma stood. "Thanks for coming to get them and for keeping them a second night this week."

"I don't mind. This is a big night, and from what you told me, you have a lot to do in the next couple of hours."

"That's a fact. I promise I won't be too late picking them up in the morning."

She chuckled. "Don't rush on my account. You do what you need to do. They'll be fine." She studied him with a look that seemed to penetrate his soul. She'd always been good at that. "How are you?"

Randy didn't answer right away. She expected, and deserved, more than a quick brush-off answer. "Relieved, grateful, and, even though the conclusion of tonight's festivities is pretty much a given, more than a little nervous. I've"—he nodded to the kids in the backseat—"we've all waited for this day to get here."

"It could have happened sooner."

Randy ducked his head. She was right. "I know, I just...I had to put the kids first. Not because I didn't trust Maggie, but I've seen the legal system abused. That's not easy to get over. Honestly? Now that everything is good, I keep waiting for the next obstacle."

"You guys have been through the wringer. I'm praying for smooth sailing from here to the altar."

"Thanks." He patted the top of the car. "I gotta get busy. It's a thirty-minute drive out to the property. I have to set the stage before I come back here to meet Maggie. I want everything to be perfect. She more than deserves it."

Grandma raised her eyebrows. "You've concocted this elaborate plan, and you aren't picking her up?"

"Trust me, I offered, but she had a nail appointment or something. Since she was already out it made more sense for her to come here."

She rolled her eyes heavenward. "Kids these days. No sense of romance."

"I'm pretty sure my reputation as a romantic will be secure after tonight. Tell Grandpa thanks again for letting me borrow his pickup and stuff."

"I will."

Randy watched her drive away. When she turned the corner, he rubbed his hands together. "Let's get this show on the road." He went to the back of the truck and did a quick inventory. Logs for the fire pit, a shovel, a step ladder, a heavy-duty extension cord, both of his patio loungers, half a dozen boxes of twinkle lights, and two heavy throws. There was also a picnic basket with an assortment of finger foods and a thermos of hot chocolate.

For once, the crazy Oklahoma weather had cooperated. There wasn't a cloud in the sky, and none were expected. On top of that, it would be well after midnight before the temperature dropped below fifty.

Randy didn't know why Maggie loved meteor showers so much, but tonight's show promised to be memorable in more ways than one. Just to reassure himself, he opened the cab of the truck and checked the glove box. The ring was there. He lifted the lid of the little velvet box and turned it this way and that, watching it sparkle in the January sun. His mouth went dry when he imagined finally slipping it on Maggie's finger.

He got in the truck and drove out to the old Cooper place. The pond on the property had been a favorite fishing place for his grandpa and him for a lot of years. He couldn't wait to bring his son out here next spring to further the family tradition.

His son. His daughter.

His wife.

This was really, finally going to happen.

His heart swelled with gratitude. *Thank You, Father.*

The old dirt road leading to the pond was pitted and rougher than he expected. For a moment he had doubts about his choice. He didn't think he'd ever been out here in the winter. What if...?

His what-ifs faded away when the bumpy trail opened into the clearing he remembered. Now, instead of knee-deep grass and the shade of dozens of old trees, he was met with a carpet of brown leaves and bare branches that would give them an unobstructed view of the sky.

For the next two hours, Randy worked to bring his vision to life. He shoveled debris from the fire pit and laid out the fresh wood. Mr. Cooper had promised to drive out on his four-wheeler and light it when Randy called to let him know he was on the way back. He arranged the loungers so that he and Maggie would have the best view of the northern sky. He hung the lights in the closest trees, switched them on, and stepped back to watch them twinkle. In the gathering twilight, it looked like the stars had come down to live in the bare branches.

A small shiver twitched at his shoulders. Randy ignored it. It was more anticipation and nerves than temperature. Between the fire, the throws, the cocoa, and the snuggling, they'd be plenty warm out here for a couple of hours. He couldn't wait to see the look on Maggie's face when he rounded that last corner and brought her into his version of a winter wonderland.

Maggie grabbed the handle above her head as the truck bounced and rocked. "Where are we going?"

"Sorry," Randy answered. "Winter hasn't been kind to this road. Just hang on. We're almost there."

"The term *road* is a bit generous, don't you think?" Maggie asked as the truck swerved to miss something she couldn't even see.

Randy straightened the wheel and glanced her way. "Close your eyes."

The pickup was barely crawling now. The reduced speed didn't make the ride any smoother. "No way. If I'm going to die, I want to see it coming."

Randy brought the vehicle to a stop. "You're adorable when you bicker, but we aren't going a single inch farther until you close your eyes and promise to keep them closed until I tell you to open them."

Maggie faced him. There was something different about him tonight. Something in his expression that made mush of her insides.

Was tonight the night? Finally?

Women's intuition or wishful thinking?

Did it matter?

All that mattered was that the agony of the last two weeks was over. That she was right where she wanted to be with the man she loved with all of her heart. The betrayals and heartbreaks of Jack and Cameron were never far from her mind, but Randy was different.

Tonight was different.

Maybe, just maybe tonight would be the night that brought her one step closer to a man she could trust and a future she could believe in. The thought made her giddy with hope.

Maggie took a deep breath, cinched her seatbelt, and closed her eyes as tightly as she could. "Your wish is my command."

"No peeking."

She etched a cross over her chest and grabbed ahold of the dash when she felt the truck gain a little speed. Everything in her wanted to squint them open just a hair. He'd never know, but she would, and as much as she wanted to look, she wouldn't ruin his surprise.

The truck lurched to the side, and bounced to a stop.

"Keep them closed," Randy said. "I'm coming around to open your door."

Maggie had never wanted to open her eyes so badly in her entire life. She bounced in the seat. "All right, all right, but hurry. The suspense is killing me."

The seat shifted. Maggie thought Randy was getting out, but instead, she felt his lips against her eyelids.

"You really are the most beautiful woman in the world."

Oh, this man melted her heart. Before she could respond she heard his door open.

"Now keep them closed."

She frowned in his direction and pointed to her eyes. "You've got about sixty seconds before willpower is out the door."

"Beautiful, but testy."

"Fifty-nine, fifty-eight..."

His door slammed, and she heard the sound of his boots crunching through dried leaves just seconds before her door opened.

"Give me your hands. I'll help you down."

Maggie did as he instructed and scooted to the edge of the seat. There, she hesitated. As much as she trusted him, this whole thing was a little disorienting.

"Here," he said. She felt hands on her waist and after a second of weightlessness her feet found the ground.

"There you go, safe and sound." He snuck a quick kiss before he turned her loose and tucked her hand in the bend of his arm. "We're going to take about twenty steps. Just let me lead you."

Maggie snuggled close to his side. "I'm all yours."

"I like the sound of that."

Sensations surrounded Maggie as they walked. She could hear crackling and popping. A flicker of light against her eyelids combined with a smoky smell that twitched at her nostrils. There was a fire close by. A few steps farther and she began to feel its warmth.

Randy stopped and pulled her into his arms. She felt his mouth next to her ear. "Open your eyes," he whispered.

All of the sensations of the previous few seconds coalesced into reality.

"Oh, Randy." Maggie pulled out of his embrace and turned in a slow circle, enthralled by the spectacle around her, touched by the work it represented. The flickering fire in the pit and the twinkling lights in the trees turned the barren winter clearing into a fairy tale. Maybe her happily-ever-after was more than wishful thinking.

"Surprise."

"It's magical," she whispered. "Oh, look!" She pointed at the sky as something streaked toward the earth so bright she could almost see the smoke in its wake. "A falling star. Did you see it?" She closed her eyes.

"What are you doing?"

"Making a wish. Daddy always said that a wish on a falling star was a sure thing."

"In that case, I hope you brought your wish list for the next decade."

"What do you mean?"

"Did you miss the announcement?" Randy led her to one of the loungers positioned next to the dancing fire. "Word is we're in for a spectacular meteor shower tonight." He settled her into one of the chairs, tucked a throw around her legs, and opened the picnic basket. "Hot cocoa?"

Maggie stared at him. This whole thing was beyond her wildest dreams. And he'd done it all for her. No one had ever loved her like this. "Is there anything you didn't think of?"

"I aim to please."

"Then yes, please. Cocoa sounds wonderful."

He brought out a couple of travel mugs, filled them to the brim from a thermos, and handed one to Maggie.

She took a cautious sip. "This is good."

"My own special recipe." Randy sat on the edge of the second lounger. "You warm enough?"

"Perfect. This whole thing is perfect."

"Good. They promised quite a show, and I wanted to watch it with my best girl."

His words brought tears to her eyes with such force that she could hardly hold them back.

"Whoa..." He leaned forward and used a gloved finger to wipe them away. "I didn't mean to make you cry."

Maggie looked up at the sky and tried to get her suddenly fractured emotions in check. "Just a stray memory I wasn't expecting."

"Want to share?"

"It's silly."

Randy wrapped one of her gloved hands in his and brought the wooly knuckles to his lips. "Try me."

"My dad used to call me his best girl when I was small." Another sting of betrayal nipped at her heart. Why couldn't her father have supported her when she needed him the most? Why had he pulled away from her and stayed gone? Why did men come and go in her life with so little thought for her feelings? When she glanced in Randy's direction, her heart warmed. Here was a guy who could be trusted with her heart. "He's the reason I love stuff like this so much."

"Really?" Randy shook out the second throw and stretched out on his own lounger. "I wondered where that came from."

"Dad was an amateur astronomer. We used to sit on the back porch with his star charts and a telescope. I've seen the moons around Jupiter and the rings around Saturn. He showed me the constellations and taught me their names. The universe is so vast, and there's so much out there." She sighed. "Sorry, I get a little carried away."

"Not at all," Randy said. "You're normally so grounded, so

focused on the here and now and what has to be done next. I know that your relationship with your parents is strained. It's nice to see this side of you. To know that all the memories aren't bad."

"No, they're not. Baking with Mom, stargazing with Dad. Then I grew up and decided I could run my own life. I guess I got ahead of myself there."

"Maybe not as much as you think. I've never seen anyone work toward a goal as hard as you have. I'm beyond proud of you."

Randy was certainly not Cameron or Jack. Maybe the hesitation that had confused her so much had been her imagination. "Thanks for being my cheerleader for all these months. Thanks for never losing faith in me the last couple of weeks. Knowing that you believed in me was all that kept me going. Oh..." They both watched in silence as a half dozen new lights flared to life overhead. "I know you worked hard on this, but could we turn off the lights? We'll be able to see the sky better."

"Sure." Randy left his place on the lounger, and a few seconds later the lights winked off. "Better?" he asked when he returned.

"Much." Maggie pointed. "Look, there and there. They're starting to come faster now."

Randy gazed where she directed.

They watched in silence a few moments. "I have one particular memory of Dad and me out on the back porch. We watched as the meteors fell like silver rain. It was the most spectacular thing I'd ever seen. I've never witnessed another like it."

Suddenly the sky came to life with dozens of fiery streaks.

"Until now." Her whisper was awestruck as meteors fell so fast that she wasn't sure where to look next.

"Wow, would you look at that?" Randy sat up as if to see better. "Heavenly fireworks, how appropriate."

"Isn't it amazing?" Maggie's gaze was glued to the sky. "Thanks for doing this for me." When Randy didn't answer, she pried her eyes from the celestial show to see what he was doing. Her breath caught in her throat and her eyes filled when she saw him beside her on one knee, an open ring box in his hands.

"I never doubted you for a second," he said. "There is nothing in that sky as beautiful or as precious as you. I've waited so long for this day to come. I know that marriage is for better or for worse. Hopefully, the worst is behind us. Maggie Janelle Hart, will you marry me?"

Every dream Maggie had for her future narrowed down to this single point in time. She tried to speak, to tell him how much she loved him, but the only word that could sneak past her constricted throat was a shaky "Yes."

Randy stood and held out his hand. Maggie took it, and he pulled her to her feet. His eyes never left hers as he worked the glove off her left hand and slid the ring onto her finger. The sky continued to rain light around them as he pulled her into his arms. When his lips met hers, Maggie's heart burst free like one of the meteors, bright and glowing and full of fire. She simply melted into his arms and allowed the fire to consume them both.

It was almost midnight by the time Randy and Maggie returned, hand in hand, to the truck. They hadn't seen a meteor in thirty minutes, and the temperature was dropping rapidly.

"I love that you did all of this for me." Maggie held up her ring. "I'll never forget this night as long as I live. But you're gonna be worthless in class tomorrow."

He opened the door for her. "Don't worry about me. I took a vacation day." He glanced over his shoulder. "But I do need to come out here bright and early and clean up our mess."

"Let's do that now," Maggie suggested. "What will take you a couple of hours to accomplish we can have done in no time.

It's supposed to be cold again tomorrow, and I'll feel horrible thinking about you out here by yourself."

"It'll be OK."

"No, it won't." Maggie turned and headed back to the clearing. "You start taking the lights down. I'll get the chairs."

"Bossy much?" Randy asked.

She chuckled as she bundled up the throws and folded the chairs. "Just taking care of my man." Maggie stacked the chairs and stuff into the back of the pickup while Randy tackled the lights. In less than an hour, the clearing was free of evidence of their visit, all except the smoke drifting from the extinguished fire pit.

Randy opened the door again and kissed her before he handed her up into her seat. "Thanks. You were right. It feels nice to know that I don't have to come back out here tomorrow."

"I told you so," Maggie said as he climbed into his seat. "It won't take us long at all to unload everything at your house. Then we can both rest knowing that the mess is all put away."

"I think I can handle it from here."

She gave him a long stare, and he cringed. "All right already. Gee, you're relentless." But he was grinning when he said it.

"It just makes sense." She leaned across the seat and placed a quick kiss on the side of his face. "If we're going to be a team, a family, it should start now. Besides, it gives me a few more minutes with you. I'm not quite ready for the magic of this night to end."

Randy leaned across the console, caught her face in his hands, and brought her mouth to his. When he released her from the kiss, he said, "I don't have words for how much I love you. I can't wait until we're a family. Max and Mariah mean the world to me." He put the pickup in gear and started the bumpy drive to the blacktop.

Maggie didn't mind the jolts and potholes nearly as much

on the way out as she had on the way in. It was hard to be annoyed when all of your wishes and dreams were finally coming true. She spent the thirty-minute drive back to Randy's house snuggled in her coat, thinking about the details of the intimate wedding they'd agreed on months before.

When they reached his house, they each carried a lounger to the back porch before returning to the truck to load up with the smaller things. Randy tucked the lights into the picnic basket, and Maggie grabbed the throws and followed him into the house.

"You keep these stacked on the trunk at the foot of your bed, right?"

"Yep." He shook the thermos. "You want a final cup of cocoa before you head home. I can heat up the leftovers in the microwave."

"Sure. I'll be back in just a second." Maggie went down the hall, turned on the light to his room, and took the time to shake the throws out and refold them. The motion of the air sent a bundle of papers on the edge of his dresser drifting to the floor. She picked them up, but before she could replace them, words jumped out at her.

Vacation.

Adoption.

Dread settled in Maggie's middle as she flipped through the stack. There were several printouts filled with pictures of sandy beaches and attractions from Galveston and Padre Island. A glance at the traveler information turned her mouth to cotton. Number of guests...three. She cut her gaze up the hall. Who was he planning to leave at home? Something in her heart assured her it wasn't one of the kids.

Hurt laid her heart bare as she looked at the time stamp on the bottom of the pages. Monday night. The night Samantha Archer's call had upended everything. Maggie groaned as Cameron's and Jack's faces flitted through her memory. They'd left her when she needed them the most. And Randy? Was he just the latest man to cut and run when things got tough. Only this one had planned to take her kids with him.

Next came page after page of information on how to adopt a foster child. One printout in particular caught her attention.

Suspension of parental rights.

The inked in portion below was smudged but Randy's handwriting was plain enough. The word stole her breath.

Unfit.

Maggie closed her eyes as Sophie's words replayed in her mind.

Haven't you figured out that you're just a means to an end?

But that couldn't be right. He'd just proposed. He loved her. Why would he...?

Randy could never love someone like you. He just wants Max and Mariah.

No, that couldn't be true.

I can't wait until we're a family. Max and Mariah mean the world to me. His own words this time. Had he waited to propose to see if she'd be charged with a crime? Had he proposed now because that wasn't an option and marriage was the only way to get what he really wanted?

Despair clogged her throat and the papers crinkled in her hands as she gathered her strength and marched to the kitchen.

"What are these?" She tossed the papers on the bar, where they skittered in six directions.

Randy looked up from pouring their cocoa. He scooped up the papers and glanced at them.

She stared at him. How could his expression be so unconcerned?

"Nothing."

She couldn't find words through the fury. He must have deciphered the look on her face.

"It's not what you think."

"Seems pretty straightforward to me."

Randy took a step toward her, but she backed up.

He held his hands out to his sides as his expression finally caught up to the gravity of the situation. "I panicked, OK? When Samantha called me a couple of nights ago, the situation seemed out of control. She was talking about *years* before we could get our lives back on track. All I could think about was you going to jail, and God forbid, some stranger ending up with your...*our* kids. If I had them, if I could talk you into making them legally mine, then they'd be safe until you could be a part of their lives again."

"Yeah, and that certainly explains why you've hesitated over our plans for the last two weeks. I thought you were just waiting to see how this all played out. It hurt, but I could understand how hard it might be to think of a wedding when there was a chance I was going to jail." Maggie looked at him, accusation in her eyes. "But you were waiting to see if you could get the kids without being shackled to me." She twisted the ring off her finger and plopped it on the bar between them. "It'll be a cold day in a hot place before you take my kids. They're coming home Monday night. You make sure you send all of their stuff with them. All of it." She turned and rushed from the room, grabbing her coat and bag on the way to the door. She had to get out of there before he had a chance to touch her. If he touched her right now, she'd die.

CHAPTER SIXTEEN

THREE DAYS, and she still cried a dozen times a day.

Three days, and she still didn't know how she was supposed to live with her dreams smoldering in a heap at her feet.

Three days, and she still didn't know how she could have been so gullible a third time.

Three days, and she still couldn't believe it was over.

Maggie sat on the edge of her bed Monday morning and forced herself to keep her eyes open. Four nights with nothing but snips and snatches of sleep made that nearly impossible.

How could she have been so gullible? How could he have used her so completely?

Questions that had no answers.

Sorrow where there should have been such joy. Today was the day she went back to work. And as much as she'd longed for that, the day would get even better. She hugged her arms around herself. After eighteen months of jumping through every hoop CPS could throw into her path, Max and Mariah were coming home tonight.

She rubbed her grainy eyes, pushed herself to her feet, and clamped down on a new spate of tears that threatened to bring her morning to a standstill. Randy might have betrayed her in the worst way possible, but that wouldn't stop her from making tonight as special as she could for her babies.

Maggie carried her phone into the kitchen, taking it off silent mode as she walked. The little 10 over the phone icon and the 6 over the text message icon made her glad she'd kept her notifications off. She didn't even have to look to know who they were from.

While her coffee brewed, she paged through the notifications. All Randy. At least he hadn't left any more voice mail messages since the last time she'd checked. Every time she heard his voice, her heart threatened to break all over again. She deleted them all. What was the point?

They were done.

Tears begged for release, but Maggie pressed her fingers to the corners of her eyes and forbade them passage. She had lots of practice in overcoming the hurt. A few days of hard work. A few days occupied by the routine of getting her babies home and settled, and Randy would be a part of her past, just like Cameron and Jack.

Good luck with that.

She ignored the sarcastic voice in her heart and scrolled for Ember's number. That was one more thing she didn't think she could handle today. No way would she be able to hide this bone-deep hurt from her friends at the craft store. If there was a side to take, she knew they'd take hers, but Maggie didn't think she could stand the sympathy in their eyes. At least she had a valid excuse for playing hooky.

"Hey Maggie, you're up early," Ember said when she answered the phone.

"You too."

Ember laughed. "Life as a mother and a business owner doesn't offer many opportunities to sleep in. What's up."

"I need to skip the meeting today." Despite all the promise of the day, she still had to take a moment to force some enthusiasm into her voice. "I'm going back to work this morning, and Max and Mariah are coming home tonight. I need some extra time around here to get ready."

"That's wonderful news, Maggie. I know you must be on cloud nine just thinking about it. Oh, hang on just a minute."

The next words were muffled as if Ember had her hand over the microphone. When she came back, it was impossible for Maggie to miss the laughter in her voice.

"Do you know anything about what's going on in Randy's class today? Quinn's about to take the girls to school, and Kasey tried to smuggle her goldfish out of the house in an old lunch box. She swears they're supposed to bring their pets to school today. I suppose I should be grateful that she isn't trying to take the dog."

"Pictures," Maggie said. "Randy..." Her throat clogged up at the mention of his name, and she grabbed a quick gulp of her hot coffee, blistering her tongue in the process. "I think he said something about sharing pictures of pets today."

"Well, that makes more sense. Oh, that child. Give me one more second." Obviously harried, Ember didn't bother to cover the microphone. "A picture, Kasey, a picture, not the real thing. Yes, I'm sure. Quinn, can you print her something from the computer, please?" Then back into the phone... "I'm sorry, Maggie. Don't worry about this morning. You do what you need to do. Is there anything we can do to help?"

"I don't think so. Their caseworker will bring them home this evening, and we'll be a family again."

"Worried?"

"Not really. Why do you ask?"

"Your voice sounds a little strained. I know you're thrilled, but they haven't lived with you for a year and a half. That's got to make for a few nerves."

"I'm fine. You guys just say a prayer for me."

"Of course, we will. You and Randy and those kids, you're going to make a beautiful family."

"Thanks." The word was full of emotions that threatened to betray Maggie to her friend. She swiped the call closed and collapsed into the nearest chair. There was no stopping the tears.

It wasn't supposed to be this way.

YOU MAKE *sure you send all of their stuff with them.*

Maggie's words to Randy didn't sound any better in retrospect than they had in person.

They still sounded like the end.

Like a goodbye where there wasn't supposed to be one.

Randy cleaned up the remnants of a light dinner Monday night.

His last dinner with the kids?

He couldn't entertain that thought and function. The only way to get through this was to focus on the next step. He'd have plenty of time to think about the what-ifs later.

Once the kids were gone.

Randy refused to go there until he had no other choice. Instead, he took the load of play clothes out of the dryer and folded them. He'd packed most everything else over the weekend with Max's help. The youngster was so excited to be going home, he'd never once asked why they were loading up every scrap of clothing and every single toy.

If he had asked, Randy wasn't sure what he would have told

him. Max had been bouncing with excitement and full of questions when Randy'd picked them up on Friday.

"Did you give her the ring?"

"Sure did."

"What did she say?"

Randy'd almost choked on his half-truth response. *"Yes, of course."*

Max's fist had pumped in the air. "All right!"

If God wanted to punish him for telling a half-truth, so be it. What else was he supposed to say? The kid was excited about going home. He'd find out soon enough that something was wrong. Randy would leave the dream-bursting explanations to Maggie. He rubbed the empty spot behind his breastbone. She was a pro at breaking hearts.

At eighteen months, Mariah was oblivious about what was going on. His was the only home she had a memory of. That worried him. Would she miss their bedtime routine? Would she fuss at night without their story? Would she wake up in the middle of the night, in a new place, and be afraid? As far as he knew, Maggie planned to keep her day care arrangements the same. That made him feel a little better. Routine was important for kids.

He packed those thoughts away with the clothes. Mariah loved her mother, and Maggie loved her. They'd be fine. The thought should have made him happy. Maybe it would down the road, but right now the pain was too new.

He looked at the clock. It was almost six. Samantha Archer would be here soon. With his arms loaded with laundry, Randy headed back to the bedrooms.

"Max?" he called.

A muffled voice came from the boy's bedroom. "In here, Dad."

Randy entered the room to find Max's feet sticking out from under his bed. "What are you doing?"

The little boy scooted free. Dust bunnies clung to his mop of black hair. He should move the bed and clean under and behind it. He'd have time for deep cleaning now.

Max held a baseball glove and a baseball in is hands. "Look what I found. It must have fallen back there the last time we played catch before it got cold." He tossed the ball into the air and caught it in the glove. "I guess I should probably leave this here." He grinned up at Randy. "Mom's not very good at catch. Do you remember when she tried to throw me a few last summer? She busted out the kitchen window."

Randy forced a good-natured chuckle. *This is killing me.* "How could I forget? But maybe you should put it in your suit-case. How will she get any better if you don't practice with her?"

"Yeah, I guess that's true. I can always haul it back and forth. But not for long, right?"

Randy turned away to put Max's stack of clothes on the bed, afraid that if the child was paying attention, he'd see more than he needed to. "Mm hum. Pack these clothes into your suit-case and drag everything into the living room. I need to finish with Mariah's stuff. Mrs. Archer will be here soon to take you home."

"That's silly," Max said.

"What is?"

"Why can't Mom just pick us up? We could go get pizza or something."

"It's just the way it has to be done, buddy. Finish up in here while I take care of Mariah."

Randy crossed the hall into Mariah's room. His baby girl looked so pretty in the pink ruffled dress he'd bought her for Christmas. She looked up from the corner of her crib, where she sat brushing the fur of a stuffed bear, and held out her hands. "Daddy up."

"Hey, Snooks." He packed the toys away, zipped up the suitcase, and picked up the little girl. She snuggled into his arms, rested her head against his shoulder, and put a tiny hand over his heart.

"Love here?"

Randy barely stifled a groan. It was almost more than he could bear. He put his hand over hers and whispered. "Always."

If someone had asked him two years before where he saw himself today, holding a baby girl and fighting tears because he was going to miss her smell and slobbery kisses wouldn't have crossed his mind. Right now, it was all he could do not to cry.

Instead, he prayed.

Father, I don't know if I can go back. I love these two kids so much. I love Maggie so much. How did I manage to mess things up so badly? If You can fix this, I wish You would.

Max slid into the room just as the doorbell rang. "Mrs. Archer is here."

"You sure it's her?"

"I saw her out the window."

"OK. Go let her in. We'll be right there. I just want to make sure Mariah is dry before you guys head out."

Max raced away to get the door while Randy laid the toddler on the bare changing table. A quick check told him she was dry. She was going to be ready for potty training soon. He was going to miss that—and a whole lot of other milestones—if something didn't change."

He held out his arms. "You ready?"

She reached for him. "Mama here?"

"Nope, but you'll see her soon." He snagged the bear and carried them both to the front room, where Max was entertaining Samantha with tales of his day at school.

Samantha stood as he entered the room and tossed her long dark hair over her shoulder. The smile on her face spoke of a job well done and happy endings. If she only knew the truth.

"Look at you, Miss Mariah. Don't you look pretty."

The little girl picked at the fringe of her dress. "Pink."

"Wow. Pretty and smart." She motioned to the bags stacked in the entry. "Is this all going to Maggie's?"

Randy nodded, afraid to speak.

"OK. Let's get the kiddos buckled in and then we can load up their stuff."

"I can help." Max began to roll one of his bags out the door.

"Such a big helper," she said. "Thanks."

Samantha rolled two bags, and Randy followed with a trash bag loaded with toys. They buckled the kids in and piled bags into the luggage compartment of Samantha's SUV. Randy leaned in the back door and kissed Mariah on the cheek.

"Be good, baby girl. I love you."

She gave him a wet kiss in return and jabbered something he couldn't quite translate.

He circled the car and bent to hug Max. "Mind your mom. I love you."

"I love you too." The little boy studied him with a serious expression. "Don't be sad. I'll see you in a day or two, right?"

Randy swallowed and forced the lie past his lips. "Sure thing." Was it really a lie if you were hoping to make it the truth? He straightened and closed the door.

"Sending them home is always the hardest part," Samantha said from behind him. "You've done an amazing job with these two. I know you and Maggie have plans for the future, but if you ever decide you want to give another child a home, call me. I'll hook you up."

"We'll see." Right now, his heart was too raw to even think about other kids. Maybe he'd get a puppy.

He watched as the SUV pulled from the curb and turned the corner. The tears he'd been fighting all weekend finally broke through.

It wasn't supposed to be this way.

MAGGIE ARRIVED home from work on Monday night later than she would have liked. Every patient she'd seen today wanted to hear the story about what had kept her away for so long. Knowing she'd been missed made her heart happy, but the story and the questions it generated seemed to take a little longer with each telling.

She zipped into her room, tossed her jacket and bag in the direction of her bed, and hurried back to the kitchen. Her babies were coming home, and she wanted to have a nice dinner waiting on them. Since they weren't due to be picked up until after their dinnertime, the logical part of her brain knew Randy would feed them before they left, but what if he didn't? A phone call would have answered her question, but hurt kept the phone in her pocket.

Maggie opened the pantry and felt like a contestant on "Chopped." She had thirty minutes. What could she make with boxed mac and cheese, chicken noodle soup, canned tuna, and a container of oatmeal? Maybe she should have used her extra time this morning planning dinner instead of staring out the window feeling sorry for herself.

The same lassitude that had robbed her morning returned with a vengeance and brought fresh tears to her eyes. She dashed them away impatiently.

"Stop it!"

She closed her eyes, took a deep breath, and gave herself a pep talk. "This should be one of the happiest days of your life.

You've worked your butt off to get here. It's not fair to you, it's certainly not fair to Max and Mariah, if you allow your issues with Randy to tarnish this moment. Randy is the past. Your future is almost here. Focus!"

She reached for a box of mac and cheese and a can of French cut green beans. There was half a rotisserie chicken in the fridge. It wasn't a feast, but it was quick and nourishing.

The doorbell rang, and she fumbled the box.

They're here!

Maggie put her pathetic dinner choices back on the shelf and raced to the front door. If they hadn't eaten, maybe she could just order a pizza and call it a celebration. She forced herself to slow down as she crossed the living room. Everything was neat and tidy, exactly what the social worker would be looking for. When she reached for the door, she froze. The reflection looking back at her from the mirror hanging in the entry revealed a woman with her hair tangled from a long day in and out of her jacket and eyes that were red and puffy with unshed tears.

Dinner wasn't ready, and she looked like a hot mess. What a way to greet her babies. She wouldn't blame Samantha Archer if she loaded them right back up and returned them to Randy. But it was too late to worry about any of that now.

Maggie pulled the door open and took a startled step back. The small porch was a jumble of people, but instead of Samantha Archer and the kids, Ember, Lacy, Ruthie, Piper, Sage, and Holly jostled each other for room.

Sage and Holly held matching teddy bears. One bore a pink ribbon, the other a blue one. Ember held two large pizza boxes. Lacy carried a cake. Ruthie struggled to control half a dozen large balloons printed with welcome-home messages. Piper raised a paper bag and grinned. "Ice cream," she said.

All Maggie could do was stare. "What are you guys...?"

Ember took the lead and nudged her way through the door. "Surprise welcome-home party. We knew you worked today, and we wanted to make the evening special for you and the kids. Even if they've had dinner...pizza. Are they here?"

"Not yet. I thought you were them."

"Good." Ember continued into the living room, and the others followed. "We won't stay."

Lacy kissed Maggie's cheek as she passed. "Chocolate cake. My mother's recipe. You are so blessed to get a second chance with your babies."

Piper followed. "Vanilla ice cream...sugar-free." She laughed. "I'd hate to see Max in my office tomorrow because we hyped him up on sweets tonight."

Ruthie freed a hand from the tangle of balloon ribbons and pulled Maggie into a hug. "What's wrong?"

Maggie buried her face in the older woman's shoulder and shook her head. "Not now," she whispered.

Ruthie patted her back and followed Piper into the house.

Sage and Holly brought up the rear. Maggie couldn't help but smile at the teddy bears.

"These are OK, right?" Holly asked.

"I was afraid that Max might be too old for a teddy," Sage said. "But I didn't know what else to get."

"He'll love it," Maggie assured her. She closed the door and turned to face her friends. "You guys are the best. I was late getting home. I was about to make mac and cheese and leftover chicken for dinner."

"Now you have a proper party," Piper said. "Where do you want everything?"

Maggie motioned everyone into the small kitchen. Ten minutes later, the table held a celebration dinner complete with party plates and cups. The blue bear sat in a chair with balloons and streamers for Max. The pink bear sat in Mariah's highchair with her share of the balloons.

It was all Maggie could do to keep from crying. "This is so amazing. They're going to be so surprised. I can't wait for you to meet them."

"That's not going to happen tonight," Lacy said.

"Yeah," Holly added. "We don't want to intrude on your special moment." She looked around the room and grinned. "Well, any more than we already have."

Maggie followed her friends back to the front door. "I don't know how to thank you."

"Hold them close tonight. That's all the thanks we need," Ember said as she opened the front door. "Come on, ladies."

Ruthie lingered as the rest of the group followed Ember out the door. "Could I make a pit stop before I leave?"

"Sure." Maggie pointed down the hall. "Second door on the right." While Ruthie was in the bathroom, Maggie rushed to her bedroom, ran a brush through her hair, and swiped on some lip gloss. Her eyes were still puffy, but the generosity of her friends would provide the perfect excuse if she needed one. When she came back to the front room, Ruthie waited by the door, her jacket in her hands.

"I know we don't have a lot of time, and I don't want to barge into your business, but you girls are like my own. Tell me why there are sad tears in your eyes instead of happy ones."

Maggie crossed to the front window and twitched the curtain aside. The kids weren't here yet, but it couldn't be much longer. She released the fabric and turned to face Ruthie. "Randy and I broke up a couple of nights ago."

"Oh, sweetheart. What happened?"

"Just another man I can't trust."

"Maggie..."

Things had happened so fast between Monday night's

devastating call from Samantha Archer and Tuesday's morning reprieve from Dianne Murphy. Other than the charges being dropped, Maggie hadn't had a chance to share the specifics with her friends. She did that now along with the details of Randy's proposal and the revelations that followed.

"He's been saying for weeks how much he believed in me, how much he trusted me, how he couldn't wait for us to be together." Maggie snorted. "Then things got tough." She shrugged. "It was never me he wanted. Turns out it was all about the kids."

"What?"

"Oh, he tried to explain it away, but..." She wrapped her arms around herself, not sure there was anything else to say.

Ruthie studied Maggie for a few seconds before she responded. "You know I love you. I wouldn't hurt your feelings for anything, but if you can't see how much that man loves you, you need to take a closer look."

When Maggie didn't answer, Ruthie continued. "Who bailed you out? Who went to bat for you with Liz? Who got dragged in for questioning when Liz disappeared? Seems to me if all he wanted was your kids he wouldn't have done any of those things. All he had to do was let you twist in the wind."

"He wouldn't..."

"Exactly," Ruthie said. "You told us about Jack and Cameron. I can understand, with those experiences, why you would have a hard time trusting another man. I can see where Randy's actions would feel like another betrayal." She paused and when she spoke again her words cut right to the chase. "Do you love him?"

Maggie bit her lip.

I won't cry, I won't cry, I won't cry.

Neither would she lie. "Yeah."

"Then listen to his story."

"Story?"

Ruthie nodded. "You have a story that makes you jump to some serious conclusions about men." She crossed the room and wrapped Maggie in a hug. "Maybe he has a story too. One that pushed him over the edge and gave him pause where there shouldn't have been any." She pulled back, put a finger under Maggie's chin, and lifted her face. When their eyes met, she continued. "We all have a story, Maggie. Don't sell your future down the river until you've heard his."

CHAPTER SEVENTEEN

MAGGIE OPENED her eyes to a greedy wash of light coming through the bedroom windows. She jerked upright in the bed.

Light?

That wasn't right. What time was it? Why hadn't her alarm gone off? She threw the blanket aside, scrambled from the bed, and searched for her phone. Once she found it, she thumbed it to life.

Seven-thirty?

She was an hour and a half late.

She had to be at work in thirty minutes.

She had to get Mariah to day care and Max to school.

Her boss was going to kill her.

Maggie rushed to her closet while she punched in the number for the hospice office. As the rings counted off, she tried to formulate a plan. If she scrambled eggs for breakfast, Mariah could feed herself. Her daughter wasn't likely to be happy without her chocolate-flavored cereal, but..."

"Good Life Home Health Care. How may I help you?"

"This is Maggie Hart. I need to speak to Sheila."

"I'm sorry. Sheila isn't in the office right now. May I take a message?"

With the phone braced between her ear and her shoulder, Maggie yanked a fresh pair of scrubs from their hanger. "Yes, please let her know that I called. I'm running late, but I'll be in for my patient assignments just as soon as I can." Silence greeted her request. "Hello...are you still there?" She pulled the phone away to make sure the connection was still live.

"Yes, I'm here."

Maggie heard the faint words and put the phone back to her ear. "Good. I'll—"

"You realize it's Saturday, right?"

Saturday?

Maggie sank down to the edge of the mattress and lowered her head into her hands. She mentally scrolled back through the madness of the last few days and realized, as embarrassment heated her face, that the receptionist was right.

"Oh, right. No message then. Sorry." She swiped the call closed without waiting for a response. With a sigh of relief, she flopped back onto the bed.

Saturday? Really? The last four days had been a blur.

Maggie'd looked forward to having Max and Mariah home for so long that she'd put that dream on a pedestal and sprinkled pixie dust around it.

The reality was a lot tougher than the dream.

It was almost funny the way things you longed for sometimes became the things you dreaded. Oh, not the kids—Maggie was soaking up every moment she spent with Max and Mariah —but the busyness of it all was making her crazy.

Her original plan had included a few days off from work to get everyone settled into new routines. Her suspension had torpedoed that idea. Now, instead of leisurely mornings filled with French toast, extra snuggles, and laughter, it was a mad dash to get three people out the door with clean faces and matching shoes. Herself included.

She'd expected a little adjustment, but not this. After all, she'd been blessed to be a major part of her kids' lives even while they lived with Randy. This was meant to be a reversal of roles, where she became the caretaker and Randy became the frequent visitor while they all worked toward something more permanent for their future. Now that wasn't going to happen, and Randy's absence was a hole in the picture that she hadn't anticipated. A void that affected everyone in the house.

Mariah had turned clingy, hanging onto Maggie like a second skin from the moment she picked her up from day care until Maggie put her to bed each night. And even bedtime wasn't a reprieve. Each night, the little girl stood in her crib and cried for her daddy until exhaustion forced her eyes to close.

Maggie'd done everything she could think of to comfort her. Nothing worked.

Max was less vocal but no less troubled. He'd asked about Randy that first night. Maggie did her best to explain, but some things were beyond the understanding of a seven-year-old. He didn't understand trust issues and betrayal. All he knew was that, once again, he'd had the promise of a father, and that father was gone. He'd come home from school three days last week with notes from his teacher. The last one had requested a meeting next week.

Maggie rolled over in the bed and pulled the extra pillow to her chest. Her aching heart was almost more than she could take. If only he'd loved her as much as he'd said.

Everyone has a story.

Ruthie's comment hadn't been far from Maggie's mind all week. She knew the words were true, but for the life of her, she couldn't think of a single thing that would justify Randy's actions.

Father, I don't know what to do. I know You have a plan in all of this, but I'm not seeing it. If You won't show me the whole plan, can You at least show me the next step?

Maggie listened for any sign that the kids were awake. When nothing but blissful silence reached her, she snuggled into the pillow and let exhaustion take her.

THE MATTRESS SHIFTED, and a warm body snuggled in next to Maggie. She didn't open her eyes, wasn't sure how long she'd actually been asleep. It didn't matter. All that mattered was the feel of her son next to her. After four days of nearly constant conflict, this was a dream come true.

"Are you awake?" he whispered.

"Um hmm." Maggie pulled him closer and let his warmth wash away some of the pain of the last year and a half. They'd missed too many moments like this.

"Guess what?" Max asked, his voice low but full of excitement.

Maggie cracked one eye open. "There's a dinosaur in the living room?"

Max giggled. "No."

"You found a thousand dollars in your closet?"

"Not even. It snowed."

Both eyes came open, and Maggie realized that the light in the room hadn't changed much since she was up earlier. She'd been in such a panic about being late, she hadn't even looked outside. "Really?"

"Yeah, a whole bunch, and it's still going. Can we go out in it?"

Maggie grinned. "Might want to have some breakfast first."

"Yeah, but after.

"I don't see why not." Maggie kissed his sleep-tousled hair, released him, and sat up. She looked at her phone to get the time. It was just after eight, which meant she'd been asleep for less than thirty minutes. But she felt amazing. How could that skimpy little nap do more for her than the whole night?

"Can we have a snow day like you promised?"

Maggie dodged Max's question with one of her own. "Is Mariah awake?"

"I don't think so." Max bounced out of the bed and pulled her hand. "Come look."

Maggie allowed him to pull her to the window. Sure enough, the snow was falling in big fluffy flakes, and from the look of the yard, they already had a good four inches. She dropped the curtain. "Snow day it is. Let's get Mariah up, make breakfast, and see what the weatherman has to say."

"Yippee!"

Max raced from the room just as Mariah made her presence known. Maggie hurried into her daughter's room and lifted her from the crib. A quick feel of the toddler's diaper had her putting her back in. "You're soaked. Let's get you changed."

"Eats?"

Maggie laughed at the question. This child always woke up hungry. "We'll eat in a bit."

Mariah fussed at the delay, but Max hurried to fill her in on the day ahead. "Don't cry. It's a snow day. We get to make a snowman and go sledding and have snow ice cream." He stopped to breathe and looked up at Maggie. "Hot chocolate too?"

"We'll need some hot chocolate after all of that."

"And hot chocolate," Max told his sister because it couldn't be true until it came from him. "Is it too early to call Dad?"

Maggie's hands froze on the diaper tapes. "Dad?"

"Yeah, we can't do snow day without Dad. He has the sled."

Maggie closed her eyes, aware that her next words were going to ruin the few happy moments they'd shared. "I don't think Randy has time to do snow day today. I'll see if I can borrow a sled from someone."

Max's eyes filled with tears. "You promised," he yelled. "How do you know he doesn't have time? You didn't even ask him. Dad always has time for me. You're just mean." He glared at her. "I. Want. My. Dad!" He ran across the hall to his own room and slammed the door.

Maggie bit her lip and reached for Mariah, but the little girl rolled away and pulled her blanket over her head. A second later her wails of "Daddy" filled the room.

At her wits end, Maggie left her children in their rooms and went to get coffee. She fixed her cup and slumped into one of the kitchen chairs. She'd been manipulated by a seven-year-old. No wonder he'd been so happy about the snow. It wasn't about snowmen or sleds. It was about seeing Randy, and she'd walked right into it. It seemed a lifetime ago since they'd made that snow-day promise.

She'd forgotten about it.

Max hadn't.

And now they were back to square one...or maybe square negative three hundred twenty-eight. She'd lost count.

The voice of her conscience prodded her.

Call him. You did make a promise, and he probably misses the kids. Think about how you felt when they were taken away from you. It's just for a couple of hours, and it'll make the kids happy.

Maggie wrapped her chilled fingers around her warm mug, sipped, and fell into the insecurities she'd wrestled all week. Was she doing the right thing or just making a bad situation worse? Just because she didn't want to see Randy right now didn't change the fact that the kids needed him. But if she called him, wouldn't that do more harm than good? Wouldn't it raise false hopes for everyone? The truth was she was dying inside, right along with her kids. She was desperate to see him, to hear his voice, but wasn't it better to keep the break clean?

The truth will set you free. You need to hear his.

Not her conscience this time but the whisper of her Heavenly Father. She sat up in her chair. She needed to hear Randy's truth, Randy's story?

Everyone has a story. Ruthie's words circled in her mind once more.

Maggie didn't see how there could possibly be a story good enough to justify his actions, but what if there were? She wouldn't know if she never gave him a chance. Was she willing to miss it? Was it possible she was sacrificing her future—Max and Mariah's future—on a misunderstanding?

You'll never know until you call him.

Her conscience again, and it wasn't quite finished.

It's been a week. You're miserable, your kids are miserable. Stubbornness isn't getting you anywhere. Maybe if you cut everyone a little slack, things would get better.

Why did her head always know more than her heart wanted to accept?

Maggie stared at her phone, willing it to ring. If he called her, it would feel a lot less like surrender. But he'd gotten the hint. She'd ignored about a gazillion calls and messages, but none of them since she'd gotten the kids back. Seemed he'd given up.

"Oh, good grief." He probably wouldn't come anyway, and then she'd have that to explain to Max, but at least she'd have tried. Maggie snatched up the phone and hit his number on the speed dial before she could lose her nerve. The phone rang one time before he answered.

"Maggie?"

She closed her eyes at the sound of his voice. The way he said her name wrapped around her like a favorite sweatshirt fresh from the dryer. For a second, she couldn't breathe because her heart was pounding so furiously.

"Maggie, is something wrong?"

She finally found her voice. "No... I mean yeah." She fumbled to a stop and started over. "No, nothing is wrong, but Max, well..." She tried to force some humor into her words in an effort to disguise the neediness she hoped only she could hear. "When he saw the snow this morning, he asked about the snow day we promised him. I know this is last minute and you probably don't have time—"

"Yes," Randy said.

"Are you sure, because we don't want to impose."

"It's not an imposition, Maggie. None of you has ever been an imposition in my life. I miss them. And you." He cleared his throat before he continued. "What time should I come over?"

In spite of herself, Maggie couldn't deny the giddiness stirring at the question. The type of giddiness a five-year-old might reserve for Christmas Eve when promised a visit from Santa.

Randy was coming.

She wouldn't put out cookies and milk, but everything needed to be perfect. She had kids to feed, a house to pick up, and her hair and makeup to do. She wouldn't be found looking like she was pining away for him, wouldn't have him look at anything and think things were less than perfect, even if perfect was the last word Maggie would use to describe the week she'd had.

Inspiration struck. "Ten-thirty? We slept in this morning." That sounded better than the story of her panicked awakening. "So, we haven't had breakfast yet. Why don't I give the kids a snack?" A quick snack so she had time to paint the picture of cozy family perfection she planned for him to see. "Just something to tide them over until you get here. I'll make French toast for everyone."

"You don't have to feed me."

"I insist. A snow day needs to start with a good meal."

"OK. I'll see you in a little bit."

Maggie hung up the phone and ran for the bedrooms. "Kid's guess what?"

CHAPTER EIGHTEEN

"I LOVE YOU." But Maggie was already gone. Probably for the best. He wasn't sure she'd appreciate the words. Her call was an answer to prayer. This last week had been the longest, most agonizing of his life. He missed his kids.

His kids?

Yes, he decided. He laid back on his pillows and put his hands behind his head. Whatever happened, Max and Mariah would be his kids until the day he died. There had to be a way to take advantage of the opportunity this day represented. A way to make Maggie understand that he hadn't meant to hurt her.

Tell her about Tait.

The words landed like a gut punch.

Tait?

Twelve years later, the very name still had the power to make his heart cringe. He didn't talk about Tait to anyone. Memories and images flooded Randy's mind. Tait was the reason he'd become a foster parent. Guilt over his selfishness was the driving force behind his hesitancy with Maggie. He hadn't wanted to make the same mistakes twice.

Randy stared at the ceiling, conflicted. Maybe she did need to know, but if he told her the story now, it would just sound like a pitiful attempt to excuse his actions, wouldn't it? He rolled to his feet, wishing for the thousandth time that his dad hadn't bailed on his family. He might be twenty-nine, but sometimes he just needed to talk things out with someone who understood him and his motivations.

Mom was out of the question. She'd never liked Maggie. The news that Maggie'd been cleared of the charges had received nothing but an unconcerned grunt in response. Without another thought, he dialed the number of the person who'd never failed to be there for him. He smiled when his grandma Callie answered the phone. She couldn't have been up long, but she sounded fresh and ready to tackle the day.

"Hey, Grandma. Have you got a few minutes?"

"I have all the time in the world for you."

Her words soothed something on the inside of him that had been ruffled for a week. "Maggie called. I'm going over to spend the day with her and the kids."

"That sounds promising."

"I hope so. We promised the kids a snow day a few weeks ago. Apparently, Max hasn't forgotten. I need your advice about something."

"You know I'll help if I can."

He took a deep breath. "I feel like I should tell Maggie about Tait."

There were a few seconds of silence. "I'm surprised you haven't already."

Randy shrugged as if she were standing in front of him and not in her own house across town. "It just never came up. I'm worried that if I tell her now, she'll think I'm just trying to make excuses for my behavior."

"Are you?"

The question took him aback. "No! I wouldn't do that."

"Sweetheart, I know how much you've suffered this last week. Didn't you tell me a few weeks ago that she'd shared the story about Max's and Mariah's fathers with you?"

"Yes."

"You told me how that story helped you put some perspective on some of the trust issues she has with men. Helped you see her feelings for you in a new light. Relationships...good ones...are built on mutual trust and honesty. She was honest with you, even though it must have cost her some pride to bare her soul."

"And I loved her more for it."

"Exactly. And she deserves the same level of honesty from you. It might be the only thing that can win her back. Not the details of the story, but the fact that you trusted her enough to tell it. When are you supposed to be there?"

"In an hour or so."

"I'll tell you what. I'm going to pray about this right now. I'll ask Him to give you wisdom and direction. That if telling her is the right thing, He'll let you know. Why don't you do the same? God won't steer you wrong."

Randy didn't tell her that it felt like the idea had come from God in the first place. "That'd be great. I love you."

"I love you too. Now spruce up. You've got a family to claim."

"HE'S HERE!" Max bolted for the door before the chime of the bell had faded. Maggie followed, with Mariah in her arms, at a more sedate pace, taking the time to give the room the same sort of once-over she had before opening it to the social worker earlier this week. On Monday, she'd wanted Samantha to see a tidy and neat home prepared for her kids. Today, it was all about what she *didn't* want her guest to see. She didn't want Randy to have a clue about how overwhelming the last four days had been. She didn't want him to catch any hint about the conflict that had roosted in his absence. She didn't want him to see anything except the well-structured lie that she could get along without him just fine.

Max threw the door open and launched himself at Randy. "Dad, I told Mom you'd come. She said you probably didn't have time, but I told her you would."

Before Randy had time to respond, Mariah squealed, "Daddy." And leaned so far out of Maggie's arms that Maggie couldn't balance the weight.

Randy lunged across the threshold and scooped her up an instant before she fell. "Snooks." He bundled the jabbering little girl close in one arm and went down on one knee so that he could draw Max in with the other. He kissed the boy's head and turned to bury his nose in the crook of Mariah's neck. "Of course I have time, buddy. I'm so glad to see you guys. I've missed you more than the cookie monster misses cookies." When Max laughed, Randy messed up his hair and finally looked up at Maggie. When his gaze met hers, she didn't miss the glaze of moisture in his eyes. Her longing to be included in that hug was nearly a physical pain.

"Maggie."

"Hi." It was all she could manage. To gain some time and composure, she motioned at the open door. "You guys are letting all the heat out."

Randy stood, managing to keep hold of both kids. He maneuvered into the living room, leaving Maggie to deal with the door and then trail behind them.

"Did you bring the sled?" Max asked.

"Of course." Randy sat on the sofa with Mariah on his knee

and an arm loosely circling Max. "I've got the perfect sledding spot all picked out."

"Yay." Max pulled away.

"Where ya going?" Randy asked.

"I need my coat and my boots."

"Boots," Mariah echoed and scrambled down to join her brother.

"Not so fast." Randy stopped him. "We've got a busy, fun-packed day, but first we need to fill up on that heavenly French toast I smell. You can't sled on an empty stomach."

"But—"

"No buts." Randy grabbed the boy, bent him backwards over one knee, and used his free hand to prod the youngster's belly. "I feel an empty spot here,"

Max convulsed in laughter.

"Here"—he tickled more—"and here." Randy grinned at Maggie while Max squirmed. "I'm thinking there's room for at least two slices of toast and a piece of bacon. What do you think, Mom?"

Maggie looked away from the wrestling match on the sofa. This was going to be harder than she'd imagined. Everything in her wanted to forget hurt feelings and harsh words and dive in and play. Instead, she crossed her arms and nodded. "At least that. You guys come on in the kitchen."

She fixed plates for everyone and watched while they ate. She might as well have been invisible where Max and Mariah were concerned, but more than once she caught Randy's gaze on her. His smile was quick each time he caught her looking. Maggie didn't know what to feel.

While Randy helped the kids get into their snowsuits, Maggie cleaned up the kitchen and prayed. *This is killing me, Father. I'm actually jealous of the way he holds the kids. All I want to do is run into his arms, but I can't. Please show me what I'm supposed to do.*

"You about done?" Randy asked from the kitchen doorway. "They're bundled up and raring to go."

Maggie took a deep breath before she turned to face him. She wiped her hands on a towel and managed a smile. "Just about. I guess I need my boots too."

"Great. I'll get them loaded in and buckled up." He paused, and Maggie could tell he had more to say, but he turned away and called to the kids as he left. "Let's get this snow day started."

For the next two hours, Maggie did her best to bury her feelings and enjoy the day. The sun came out and warmed everything up to a comfortable temperature, and she and Randy took so many turns pulling the sled up the hill that they were ready to drop by the time the French toast wore off. But the laughter of the kids, something she'd heard precious little of the last few days, kept Maggie going.

She positioned the sled on the cusp of the hill, sat on it, and took a firm hold on Mariah. "You ready?"

Mariah's answer was an unintelligible string of gibberish, but there was a very clear "yes" in the middle. Maggie glanced back at Max. "OK, give us a shove and wait right here. Randy will be back with the sled in a minute or two." Without another word, they went flying down the hill.

Randy chased after them as the sled slowed. "That was a good one."

"Yeah, but I think it's time to warm up. Why don't you go up and give Max a final ride. We'll go home for some sandwiches and cocoa."

"Sounds like a plan." Randy took the rope and set off up the hill.

"I thought I might find you here."

Maggie looked up from brushing snow off the front of Mariah's snowsuit to see Callie heading toward them. "Callie, what are you doing here?"

"Looking for you guys. Randy mentioned a snow day. This was always his favorite place for sledding." She stopped as the sled bearing Max and Randy swooshed by them. It stopped a dozen feet away, and the guys rolled off into the snow, both giggling like children.

"Grandma!" Max waded through the snow and grabbed Callie in a fierce hug. "Did you come to sled with us?"

Callie laughed. "As much fun as that might sound, I don't think so. I don't bounce as well as I used to. No, I came to see if you guys were ready for a break. I made chicken soup." She looked at Maggie and Randy. "You two look worn out."

"That's one way to put it," Maggie said.

"They can't be tired yet," Max said. "We still have a snowman to build."

Maggie groaned.

"I have an idea," Callie said. "Why don't I take the kiddos back to the house for some soup and a nap. I'm sure you two can find something to occupy your time for an hour or so."

"I don't want a nap," Max whined.

Randy stooped down beside him. "But we don't always think about ourselves, do we? Look at Mariah." Randy paused while Max did as requested. "She's tired and probably cold. Some hot soup and a rest would be good for her. You don't want to build a snowman without her, do you?"

Max kicked the snow at his feet. "No." He looked up. "You promise you won't go home until we finish our day."

"I promise."

Max's sigh was heavy. "OK."

"Good," Callie said. "I've missed you. Did I forget to mention I made cereal treats?"

That got Max's attention. "The chocolate kind?"

"You'll have to come see for yourself."

Maggie helped Randy buckle the kids into Callie's car. As they loaded the sled, nerves twisted her stomach. She hadn't planned to spend any time alone with Randy today. The kids had been a comfortable buffer between them all morning. And speaking of planned, Callie's arrival had been just a little too convenient. She loved Randy's grandmother, but the woman knew how to get her way. She watched as the car, and her kids, disappeared. Now what?

"You too tired to take a walk?" he asked.

She looked up to the top of the hill. "Only if I have to go back up there."

"Nope. I saw a path over there with some benches." He held out a hand. When she hesitated, he whispered, "Please."

She took his hand but refused to meet his gaze. If he noticed, he didn't let on. He just squeezed her fingers and started walking. Around the curve of the hill, they found a path that surrounded a small pond. A sense of déjà vu unnerved Maggie. It looked a lot like the little pond from last Thursday night.

The night Randy proposed.

They walked in silence for several minutes. She didn't know what she was supposed to say, and if Randy had something on his mind, he was keeping it to himself.

"I'm sorry," he finally said.

Maggie kept walking, not sure how to respond. His actions had wounded her to the core. "Sorry" didn't fix it.

Randy sighed. "Did I ever tell you that Max and Mariah weren't my first experience with foster kids?"

She stopped and looked up at him. "You said they were your first placement."

"They were my first as a foster father, but I had some previous experience with how the system worked."

"How?"

"Tait Mosley." Randy cleared his throat. "Give me a second."

They walked a few more feet. When they reached a bench Randy brushed the snow off the seat. "Let's sit for a few minutes."

Once they were settled, he faced her. "Tait Mosley was a kid I knew in school. He transferred to Garfield right after Christmas break the year I was a junior. He was just a freshman, a skinny stick of a kid. A real loner, more interested in the sci-fi comics he carried around than friends or conversation. You've seen the type. Clothes that never seem to fit just right, a little awkward. Add in quiet and nervous, and you have a feeding ground for every bully in a twenty mile radious. I was on my way home from school one day and I saw a couple of the bigger boys in my class knocking him around. Tait was trying to get away, but they wouldn't leave him alone. I went to his rescue, told them I knew some of the cops in town and that if they didn't leave, I'd report them."

Randy stopped, seemingly caught up in his memories. "Tait was a foster child." Randy finally said. "After I rescued him, he told me all about it. He'd been in the system for years, bounced around from family to family, never finding a place to call home. Never in one house long enough to make friends. I'd grown up in a secure home with a family that loved me. I couldn't take it all in, couldn't imagine living the sort of life he described. I became his unofficial big brother that day. Sort of a...protector. I asked if I could move my locker next to his so I could keep an eye on him between classes, and I made a point to walk him home every day."

"That was very sweet of you."

"I didn't think of it like that. The kid needed someone in his corner and it felt good to have someone look up to me." His swallow was audible. "And then Tracey came along."

"Tracey?"

Randy sighed as if the memory was painful. "Tracey Badger. Tall, thin, beautiful, a cheerleader. I had such a crush. She didn't know I existed. But then one Friday I walked out of English class, and there she was. When she fell into step beside me, I almost tripped over my own two feet. When she asked if I wanted to go get a soda after school, I looked around to make sure she was talking to me. I couldn't get the 'yes' out of my mouth quickly enough."

"What about Tait?" Maggie asked.

"Where were you when I needed you?"

Randy's question might have sounded humorous to someone who didn't know him. Maggie heard the desolation in his voice.

"I thought he'd be OK for one day. But while I was enjoying a soft drink with the lovely Tracey, the boys I'd chased off earlier ganged up on Tait and beat him up."

"Oh, no."

"That's not the half of it. Tracey? She only asked me out so they could have a chance to ambush him. When I went back to school the next Monday, Tait was nowhere to be found. I went to his house after school, and his foster parents told me what had happened. It was so bad he spent two nights in the hospital, and once he was discharged, his social worker placed him with a new family in a new town." Randy released her hand and leaned forward. "I never forgave myself for being so selfish. I was out enjoying myself when Tait needed me."

Maggie jumped to Randy's defense. "You were a kid."

Randy shrugged. "Most of me knows that, but it still hurts when I think about it. I still wonder if things might have been different if I'd made better choices."

"That's a horrible story. What happened to the guys who beat Tait up?" Maggie asked.

"They walked. I never knew the whole story there, but this was the year that Nicolas joined Garfield's police department. He was good for a few answers. He told me that some charges had been filed, but one of the guys...his dad was some muckity muck in some county office, and he managed to get the charges dropped. It was all my fault and one of the worst miscarriages of justice I've ever been witness to...until they found those pills in your car."

He finally looked at Maggie. "I guess I should have told you all of this a long time ago, but it's not easy to talk about, and I didn't think it was important."

"Did you ever see him again?"

"No. I looked everywhere for him. Well, everywhere a seventeen-year-old kid can look. I even made Mom take me to the CPS office. I just wanted the chance to tell him that I was sorry I'd let him down. They wouldn't tell me anything."

"He's the reason you became a foster parent." Maggie whispered the words as some of the missing pieces began to fall into place. Tears clouded her vision. She hadn't imagined anything he could say that would make a difference. She hadn't imagined this.

"Yeah." There was pleading in his eyes when he continued. "Maggie, when this whole arrest thing happened, it messed with my head. I didn't know what I should do. I knew you hadn't done anything wrong, but I didn't know if the police could prove you didn't. It was never you I mistrusted. It was the system that had failed me once already. Max told you about the ring, didn't he?"

She nodded.

"Not asking you to marry me was breaking my heart, but I had to put the kids and their safety ahead of anything I wanted for myself. Then, when Sam called that night and said she would move the kids if I didn't take a step back...I panicked." He looked at the ground. "All I could think of was Tait and how I never saw him again. I pulled up all that adoption stuff because I couldn't bear to think about losing you and them. Deserting you was the last thing on my mind. I know my mom put the thought in your head that all I wanted was the kids. Nothing could be further from the truth. I was scared out of my mind and grasping at straws to protect what we had.

"I love you. I want our future back. That's all I've ever wanted. If you can't forgive me, I'll have to live with that, but I wanted you to know I never meant to hurt you. I'd never try to take the kids from you."

Maggie searched his face, looking for anything there that might say something different than his words. When she didn't find it, she looked up and away.

At some point in the last few minutes, it had started snowing again.

She closed her eyes and opened her heart to the story he'd told, well able to imagine how helpless he must have felt as a young man and now. Her tears fell as she got up and walked a few steps away. Everything inside of her wanted to grab ahold of him and never let go.

"I don't deserve you," she whispered.

"What?"

Maggie jumped at the nearness of his voice. He was standing right behind her, but the snow had muffled his movements. She turned and looked up at him, blinking as snowflakes and tears clouded her vision. "I don't deserve you."

Randy pulled his gloves off and used his fingers to wipe the moisture from her cheeks. "No more tears," he said, his voice gruff with emotion. "We've had enough of those to last a lifetime." He unzipped his coat and pulled a chain from under his sweatshirt. When he held it up to the light, Maggie gasped. It was her ring.

Without saying a word, Randy slipped the chain over his head, undid the clasp, and pulled the ring free. "Maggie, we've both been hurt, we both have baggage. Let's make a fresh start together." He went down on one knee. "I love you. I don't want to spend another day without you. Please say you'll marry me."

Maggie looked down at him as the snow swirled. Everything she wanted in life was just one word away. She tugged her left glove free and held out a hand that wasn't quite steady. "Yes."

Randy slid the ring onto her finger, stood, and pulled her close.

Maggie looked up into his eyes and couldn't help but smile. It was snowing harder now. Flakes dotted his hair and clung to his lashes. She was having her own special version of a snow day, and she liked it a lot.

"I love you so much," she said, "Thanks for not giving up on me."

"Never in a million years." He lowered his mouth to hers. His lips were ice cold, but the promise of the future they'd build together was all the warmth Maggie needed.

EPILOGUE

Four months later

"I now pronounce you man and wife."

Maggie hardly heard the words. Every sense she had was focused on Randy.

They'd made it.

Odds stacked against them.

Through misunderstandings and delays.

Here they were.

Randy gave her hands a gentle tug. "Come here, Mrs. Caswell."

Maggie melted into the arms of her future and lifted her face. When her husband's lips found hers for the first time, she leaned into him with a sigh of ecstasy.

This, just this, for the rest of my life.

"Yuck."

The happy couple pulled apart as the small assembly of friends and family gathered at Valley View Church chuckled at

Max's reaction. Maggie leaned her head against Randy's chest. When she got her hands on that child...

"Get used to it, buddy," Randy said.

Maggie looked at the first row of pews where Max and Mariah sat with Randy's grandma. She crooked a finger. "Come on."

The kids raced to the front of the church. Max snuggled up beside Randy while Mariah scrambled into Maggie's arms.

Pastor Sisko laughed as the new family sorted themselves out. "Ladies and Gentlemen, it is my great privilege and pleasure to present to you Mr. and Mrs. Randy Caswell...and company."

The foursome led the way back to the fellowship hall, where a small reception waited. They positioned themselves by the door and prepared to greet their friends. Mostly friends. Maggie's parents had declined the invitation due to vacation plans they couldn't...or wouldn't... change, and Sophie? Well, that relationship was going to take a lot of work. Maggie refused to give up, and she wouldn't allow it to ruin her day. She had Randy and her kids. They'd make their own family.

Callie and her husband were the first in line. She hugged them both. "I wanted to be the first to say congratulations. I love you both so much."

Benton patted Randy roughly on the back. "You did good, boy."

Callie held her hands out to Max and Mariah. "Come with Grandma, kids. Let your mom and dad have some time with their guests."

Ruthie took her place. "Look at you. I knew you'd be a beautiful bride."

"Thank you." She meant the words in about a hundred different ways. Maggie pulled the older woman in for a hug. There was something different about her lately. Some little spark of happiness that hadn't been there before her Christmas cruise. Opinion among the crafters was that she'd met a guy, but Ruthie had yet to confirm or deny. That would be a story for another day.

Ember and Quinn came next. Quinn, dashingly handsome, as always, and Ember glowing in the final weeks of her pregnancy. She patted her belly. "Boys are so ornery. When Max said *yuck*, I laughed so hard I almost peed my pants."

Maggie shook her head. "Boys are a special breed. Be afraid. Be very afraid."

Piper Goodson and her husband, Evan, stepped up as the path cleared. She grinned at Randy. "I guess I have to be nicer to you now that you're married to one of my best friends."

Randy turned it around on her. "I guess I have to love Maggie a little better now that I'm married to one of my boss's best friends."

"You two are hilarious." Maggie hugged Piper and Evan and pointed across the room. "There's cake, go get some."

As they walked away, Maggie held out a hand to Lacy and pulled the solemn woman into a hug. Lacy seemed to be spiraling deeper into her grief instead of working her way out of it. If there was anything to say, Maggie wasn't sure what it was. Instead of words, she lifted a silent prayer over her friend. *Jesus, she's so broken. Please heal her heart.* She handed Lacy on to Randy and put her arms around Lacy's husband, Cole. "I'm praying for you," she whispered.

"Thank you," Cole said before moving away.

"That was the most beautiful ceremony." Holly took Maggie's hands and bounced in place.

"She's already making notes about ideas she wants to steal... I mean borrow for hers," Sage teased.

"Borrow away," Maggie said. She could be magnanimous. Holly may have gotten her ring before Maggie, but Maggie had beaten her to the altar. But what was a little friendly competition between friends?

Twenty minutes of hugs, kisses, and well-wishes later, Maggie held out her hand to the last woman in the line. Something about the face was familiar, but she couldn't quite place her.

Maybe she was a friend of Randy's.

Recognition clicked as a grainy Facebook picture melded with the real person standing in front of her. Maggie grabbed both of her hands. "You came!"

Dianne Murphy smiled. "How could I miss it?"

"Oh, it's so nice to finally meet you. Randy, this is—"

"I know who she is." Randy bent and placed a kiss on her cheek. "Thank you is not enough."

"It was my pleasure, and since they found Liz and she's finally getting the help she needs, let's leave all of that behind us. This is a day for celebration."

"I couldn't agree more," Randy said as the music started to play. He took his wife's hand and pulled her into a hug. "May I have this dance?"

Maggie stared up at her new husband. God had kept every single promise. *Thank You, Father for having a plan for me.* She smiled up into Randy's eyes. "Each and every one for the rest of my life."

If you enjoyed Maggie and Randy's story, you're going to love reading about Lacy and Cole. Turn the page for more about Lacy: Crafted with Love, book four.

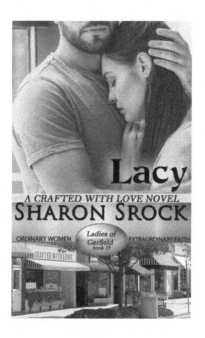

She had the perfect life, until she didn't.

Lacy Fields was so blessed, she felt like God's favorite daughter. A husband she loved, a daughter she adored, and a soon-to-be granddaughter she planned to dote on. When a tragic accident wipes away two thirds of those blessings, everything in her life comes into question. Did God ever really love her? Can she forgive the man behind the wheel? Is there life outside of her grief? Could the sick, unwanted infant she's rocking in the NICU be the answer to her prayers?

He knew she blamed him

But she'd never said so--until now. Cole Fields loves his wife, but he's out of ideas about how to help her overcome the grief of losing their only child. Her silent condemnation, her growing distance from God, and her wild plan to rebuild their family make him fear for her sanity.

Where do you go when life drags the rug out from under you...again?

Faced with another empty nursery--and a second shattered heart—Lacy is convinced that she has nothing more to give, Lacy leaves everything behind. Can Cole's prayers and God's love convince her that life is better with her in it, or will despair finally put an end to her suffering?

ALSO BY SHARON SROCK

THE COMPLETE LADIES OF GARFIELD SERIES:

Callie

Terri

Pam

Samantha

Kate

Karla

Hannah's Angel

A Makeover Made in Heaven

Iris

Mac

Randy

Charley

Jesse

Syd

Alex

Ember

Holly

Maggie

THE MERCIE SERIES:

For Mercie's Sake

Begging for Mercie

ALL ABOUT MERCIE

Made in USA - Kendallville, IN
67101_9798807923479